Bumbling Bea

by Deborah Baldwin

Published by Deborah Baldwin
Copyright 2017 by Deborah Baldwin
All rights reserved.
ISBN: 1500390356
ISBN 13: 9781500390358
Library of Congress Control Number: 2014913031
CreateSpace Independent Publishing Platform,
North Charleston, South Carolina

Dedication

To my wonderful family—
Katharine, Izzie and Craig

And *especially*
to my dear sweet husband,
Tim.

Thank you for believing in me all these years
when I couldn't believe in myself.

Independently published books need readers like you to review
us. If you'd be so kind as to write a short review and post it to
Amazon.com & Goodreads.com,
I'd appreciate it. Thanks!

Chapter One

It was Peter's fault.

"P!" I yelled to get his attention, "do I look like old Macdonald on the farm to you?"

I was splattered all over with the gross stuff. I swear it was already curdling and the entire cafeteria of students could see it. I smelled putrid--like yucky old, blackened, moldy cheese long forgotten in the back of the refrigerator. It made me wretch a little but I still managed to get in his face.

"Why don't you drink juice or water? Now I smell like I've been working in a cheese factory. You're such a dweeb, P."

When I was mad at Peter, I called him "P." He'd been P. ever since we were in kindergarten when he stuck a couple of peas up his nose and had to go to the hospital to get them out. And like those peas, the name stuck. And he was clumsy, BUT only with me. He defended himself like he always did which irritated me.

"Jeez, sorry Beatrice. I didn't mean to nearly flip over your backpack and spill two miniscule drops of lactose on your precious jacket. It was blocking the aisle between the tables like always. You are so mean these days." Peter huffed, stomping away from the lunch room.

It wasn't me speaking to Peter. It was Bumbling Bea. I've discovered I have an alter ego who I call Bumbling Bea. Strange and mean thoughts come flying out of my mouth. They didn't even sound like something I'd think or say! Bumbling Bea hadn't been around for long, but when she did rear her scary head, it was at the worst times.

One of the most memorable of times Bumbling Bea showed up was when we gave our choir director a tennis racket as a going away present. He was getting married and leaving our school. He was obsessed with tennis and was a pretty decent player. I thought it was neat, even though he had knobby knees and skinny, hairy, Minnie Mouse legs which looked kinda' weird in his way too short tennis shorts.

I thought of the present when I saw him hitting tennis balls on the tennis court after school one day. He was mumbling something and from seeing his temper in class, I figured it was about his students.

It was the first time Bumbling Bea arrived. I was class secretary for him (which made me feel super important even though he had a class secretary for every other class, too.) I thought I had power and the other kids listened to me. Bumbling Bea liked that a lot! At lunch one day I was sitting by myself, as usual. I turned to the table with the popular kids sitting behind me. "I think we should buy our music teacher a going away present since he's getting married and leaving us. How about we give him a tennis racket since he loves the game so much?"

Everyone agreed with me (which was a first) and
didn't, gave me a dollar per student donation anyway. ıı giving
money for a teacher's going away present kept you in or near the
popular kids, you gave it. And they did!

I was so excited. I checked out tennis racket prices on the internet, Dave's Discount and the hardware supply store. Dave's had the
best price. Most everything was less expensive at Dave's Discount.
My Dad told me it was because Dave bought up all the things other
businesses couldn't sell. Dad thought Dave's had good deals even
though sometimes their stuff fell apart after one use. Their price
for the tennis racket was awesome and one my class could afford.

Since I found the tennis racket right away, I had a little bit of
time left over before Dad picked me up so I looked around at the
girls' clothes. Normally, I didn't look at your typical girls' clothes
because they were always way too pink and way too fluffy. Not at
Dave's, though! I found a black and white polka dotted bikini swimming suit, matching flip flops *and* a package of panties—things were
so cheap.

"You want me to put them in a Dave's Discount box, honey?"
wondered the clerk lady who smelled like cigarettes and chewing
gum.

I heard about the Dave's Discount boxes before. People used
them to store about anything in them after they got them home: extra cat litter, broken toys, a bed for a puppy and so forth. They were
sturdy, kind of a brownish tan color with black stripes printed on
one side of them and the words "Dave's Discount" plastered over
the stripes.

Being so proud of myself for A. finding the tennis racket and
B. buying the bikini, flip flops and panties all by myself, I accepted

two boxes instead of one. I mean, they were free, you know? Dad said not to turn away free stuff if anyone at a store ever offered you anything free. I thought Dave's Discount box was one of those free things he was talking about.

"Mom, we got a deal. The racket only cost thirty-six dollars." I announced as I arrived home.

"Don't forget to take off the price tag before you wrap it, Beatrice," my mom reminded me as she whisked off to teach her art classes.

Mom! Sheesh. Sometimes she thinks I'm a baby...

My brother, Edmund, helped me wrap the box rolling it two or three times in wrapping paper and tying it with gobs of ribbons and a bunch of bows on it. We put the box in another box which went in another box. We thought it was so fun to unwrap when you received one of those sort of presents. Edmund laughed and laughed each time we played the trick on him.

This is so awesome. I said to myself. *And when I tell him I chose the present, he will think I'm one of his coolest students for doing this for him.*

That was Bumbling Bea talking. You see? Why would it matter whether my teacher thought I was the coolest student he had ever taught during his teaching career? He had thousands of kids he'd taught already and I was a lousy singer.

It was finally time to give the present. On the last day of classes before summer vacation, we usually sang through the year's music one more time. The whole choir was singing happily, but they kept turning and looking at me. I was singing loud the way I never do because I was so excited about our present. Well, *Bumbling Bea* was singing exceedingly loud because she thought I was a better singer since I thought up the present.

It was the second time Bumbling Bea appeared.

Finally, the end of the hour came and it was time for the present. I stood lifting my head proudly, "We are sad you are leaving Oak Grove Middle School. We wanted to give you something to remember us when you are off in your new life." I gave him the big box saying, "So, here is a little something to use to take out your frustrations on your new wife."

Huh? What was that I said?

I was kinda' nervous which was unusual for me and it freaked me out. So I tried again. "I meant, here's a little something to use to take out your frustrations in your new life."

Oh man. That wasn't right either.

I tried one more time, "Oh, you know when you have a bad day at your new school and want to strangle your students, you can use this instead." I cringed.

My teacher stared at me. "I don't know what you are talking about, Beatrice. I'm never frustrated with my students." He smiled at the rest of the class and ignored me.

I felt different on the inside of myself. Kinda' smart aleck-y, but I didn't know why. Maybe I was way too excited or nervous or awkward? When I am, I do dumb things to cover. It was how I felt that day. I wanted to sound grown up and cool and in charge, but I said three super dumb things to my teacher.

But I did more than say three dumb things.

Way more.

When Edmund and I were wrapping the tennis racket, Edmund's pet ferret, Bernie, got loose from Edmund's clutches and darted around my room. We were so busy screaming at Bernie that while trying to catch him, I guess my big fat foot accidentally pushed the box with the tennis racket under my bed. I picked up the other *identical* box with my new swimming suit, matching flip flops and the package of new panties and wrapped it instead.

Yes, you read it right: it was the box containing my new bikini swimming suit, matching flip flops and the new panties.

NEW PANTIES! NEW PANTIES!

But see, I didn't know it was the wrong box because I wasn't looking at my teacher when he finally opened the last box. I was busy picking up the left over wrapping paper.

Somebody whispered, "Beatrice, you left the price tag on the box."

"Embarrassing," another snickered.

THE PRICE TAG WAS SHOWING. THE STUPID PRICE TAG WAS STILL ON THE PRESENT.

I looked up and before I knew it, Bumbling Bea quipped, "There's the price tag. It shows you how much we like you and I wanted you to know all us chipped in for it."

Again with the dumb statements!

CHAPTER ONE

My teacher opened the box and there was no tennis racket.

BUT, there they were: the panties. Oh, the swimming suit and flip flops were there too, but all I saw were the PANTIES. It was as if they grew from a regular size to the size of a goal post on a football field. HUGE.

I stammered, "What? How did those get in there?"

My confused teacher said something to me, but the whole class was laughing so loudly I couldn't hear him. I grabbed back the box and ran out of class and hid in the girls' bathroom.

People called me "Panties" for days afterward until my mother heard them one too many times and threatened to call their parents.

Later I got the right present to my teacher but by then every kind of damage had already been done and I still forgot to take the price tag off the stupid present. I gave up.

Peter said later in the summer he saw my teacher hitting balls with our present tennis racket out on the court. He was back in town visiting his mother or something. I guess he hit one ball a little too hard, because the tennis racket's webbing unraveled and when it fell to the ground, the handle fell apart, too.

Yup. Bumbling Bea steps into my skin right at the wrong time. Lately, there are more times she appears than I have. Until a crazy cat ears wearing girl visiting from Japan made me see what I was doing by taking on my Bumble-Bea-ness herself. It's all a little scary when you think about it.

Chapter Two

"Next!"

Ms. Phillips' enormous voice hushed us as she swung open the backstage door. "Kids, I can see you are excited and noisy. Do you think you could keep quiet out here? At least keep it to a dull roar out here."

All of us stared at Ms. Phillips. She used our school's "established disciplinary language" on us, but we were already silent and not doing much of anything out in the hall except waiting and waiting and waiting for our turn to audition. We were lined up like lemmings waiting at the cliffs. Tiffany was curled on the floor simultaneously reviewing her French class flash cards while listening to her second e-book mystery since the morning snack break. Peter sat beside her chilling to some horrid song on his smart phone blaring so loud everyone else heard it as well.

"No sweat, Jerri," I assured her. I grabbed the dog-eared papers from my best friend's hands. Jerri was huddled in the custodian's closet by the exit door of the gymnasium. I leaned forward to Jerri whispering, "I know this backwards and forwards. Thanks for getting it, though. I've seen this play at least ten times, but I'm not too proud to cheat a little."

"No problem, Beatrice. My sister wasn't home when I lifted it from her scrapbook, but I'm sure she'd agree with you. You are the best actress to play John Smith's wife, Pocahontas. Besides, it's your last chance. Next year, we're in high school."

"Yeah, high school. And 'future' wife, Jerri," I corrected her. "They aren't married at the top of the show. Remember there's the big scene near the end when she lays on the rock in front of her tribe and begs for Smith's life? That's so cool, even though all the families in the neighborhood have seen it about ten times already."

"Next!" boomed Ms. Phillips. If she ever left teaching, Ms. Phillips could land a job on a ranch somewhere as a cowboy leading cattle across a windy prairie during a tornado. She was so loud.

"I hope you're right about auditioning last. Maybe being first in line was better?" Jerri wondered.

I muffled my answer with the pilfered script, "Jerri, I'm right about this. Okay, there are only three more kids before us. Tiffany, she's a shoo-in for a Pilgrim wife. And Peter. He's one of the only boys who is trying out other than the fifth graders Ms. Phillips dragged in here. He'll get John Smith for sure which I guess is okay since I'm gonna have to kiss him."

"Kiss? Does he know this?"

"Nah, but the kiss will make the play more believable." I added, "And there's the new girl from China. She still has to audition."

What was that I said?

I didn't have a problem with people from Japan or China. Actually, I liked people from other countries. They were way more interesting than being around people exactly like me. But I knew it sounded tough and scary to kinda dis' her.

I was nervous even though I didn't want anyone to know. I was desperate to play the lead role--the starring role in the school play. Next year, we were in high school and playing the lead would clinch being popular. Jerri was right. This was my last chance to play Pocahontas. The high school we would go to was so big. We needed all the friends we could get and building our friends list was a good plan.

Plus, bigger still was my Dad issue. Since he had moved out (Oh excuse me, "taking a break from the marriage" he said) we NEVER saw Dad anymore. The only time he ever talked to me for longer than a minute was when we talked about theater and performing. If I played Pocahontas I was assured of more than two minutes a week with Dad. Maybe he'd come to the show and see us all together and feel bad and look at our pretty mom and...

Hold it. I am getting ahead of myself. Back to my story, sorry.

"I heard you. I'm not kissing anybody." Peter sneered. "My mother made me do this. I don't want to be in this dumb thing. But if I don't, my mom said I'd have to quit working for my grandpa's lawn service. I have to keep my job. I'm saving for a scooter."

"We know, Peter. You tell us about it every other day. And Eatricebay, I think she's from Japan," Jerri corrected me.

I couldn't help feeling a little sorry for the new girl. She acted kinda' weird. Several times I had seen her standing off by herself, talking to the walls around her, bowing, and cutting the air like a karate expert. Now, you gotta admit, that's weird!

"The 'Asian' girl is no problem." I sounded more like someone else than myself. "Look at her squinting at the signup sheet. I met her at a welcome party my dad hosted for her father. He is teaching some acting classes this year at the university in Dad's department. It's some sort of exchange program. Whatever. She barely speaks English. And those cat ears she wears everywhere. Sheesh."

Okay, I took it too far and it made me feel sick inside. I laughed although I felt bad for making fun of her. What was wrong with me?

Jerri sternly glared at me. She was the sensitive one of the three of us—Peter, Jerri and I. "Have you actually heard her speak English or are you just making up things? Tiffany told me the new girl is the best reader in Ms. Phillip's Language Arts class. They were reading Shakespeare's *Romeo and Juliet* aloud and I guess she got up and acted it out before Ms. Phillips could stop her."

"So? A good reader does not an actress make," I recited. "I know I'm being sort of aggressive, but it's the way show business is. It's a dog-eat-dog world. I *deserve* the starring role. Haven't I taken dance classes since I was three and voice lessons with Madame Murphy for two years? Three times in a row I got to be the house manager at one of my dad's play productions." I looked at Jerri to see if she was still listening to me, even though she heard me recite my pathetically short resume gobs of times. I added, "Ms. Phillips won't give Pocahontas to some new girl; she's too professional to make such a stupid decision."

I didn't know if Ms. Phillips was professional, but she probably was. She certainly wasn't stupid, but my Bumbling Bea was on a roll. I felt threatened and nervous and awkward which were new feelings for me. Bumbling Bea made the snide remarks about the girl from Japan who was probably nice and tremendously talented. I was hoping she wasn't.

"Don't be too sure. Ms. Phillips has a minor in Theater. It counts for something. Besides your dad had you *usher* at his shows those three times because you begged him. You don't deserve anything special," Jerri mumbled.

Everyone needs a best friend like Jerri. She's a straight shooter, which is how my mom describes her. I can depend on Jerri to tell me the truth even when I wish she'd agree with my fib and go along with me. I've learned to depend on her honesty—kinda like a promise she gave me.

"You're next, Beatrice," Ms. Phillips appeared beside me.

"I am? Jerri?" I turned around to see my best friend escaping, running at a full gallop on the slippery waxed hallway. "Jerri was before me, Ms. Phillips."

"She's running away from us for some reason," Ms. Phillips noticed. "So, you're next. Come in. Michiko, will you please stay and read a little more for me?" Ms. Phillips asked.

The Asian girl hesitated at the door. Quietly, she returned and sat again. She bowed her head studying the script, her blue black hair hiding her round face.

Michiko is pretty, I thought. *She needs a second chance. This must be tough for her.*

She looked like one of those beautiful Japanese dolls my grandma kept on the piano in her living room. In many ways, she was elegant, with porcelain skin and small features. I felt myself softening toward Michiko. I would hate to be the new student at my school, especially from another country. If the play wasn't so important to me, I'd take back the atrocious things I said about her. Instead I opened with, "Oh yeah, your name is Michiko."

Bumbling Bea whispered to me, *Too bad. I sure hope she's ready for some real acting. No problem-o.*

I walked through the auditorium doorway stepping through a mess. In two short hours the Oak Grove Middle School auditorium became a serious disaster area. Lost notebooks, water bottles and homework assignments decorated the stage floor. Two matching jackets (probably the Sheppard twins') twisted and strangled the safety bars on the end of the bleachers. A deflated, red kick ball was smushed under a wooden stool, a grayed high top basketball shoe looking to be around a size thirteen and a half stuffed with a half-eaten banana, was thrown under the piano bench in the corner. Folding chairs were scattered across the stage. Some, flopped like dead guppies, were dented and pinched beyond repair.

"I'd like to be Pocahontas, Ma'am."

My stomach gurgled loud enough for Ms. Phillips to hear. *Butterflies*, I thought. I was nervous and anxious. This shocked me.

I was ready for this audition. I knew the script and I was an eighth grader (the oldest grade in my middle school). I deserved a big role since I had participated in the show the last two years and played measly parts. I thought nonstop about the auditions since last year's curtain closed on the play. I even kept a special calendar hidden under my old shoes in the closet. I called it my "Pocahontas Planner." It was filled with tally marks recording when I thought, read, practiced and dressed like Pocahontas. There were at least two hundred and eleven days I marked in the planner. One day I decided I would do some acting improvisation and "be" Pocahontas. I walked around the house in my mom's old bathrobe, wore a pair of brown socks impersonating moccasins and "was" Pocahontas until Mom told me to go ride my bike and get some fresh air.

Mom made my lunch on this audition day—a peanut butter and bean sprouts sandwich. She said the sprouts were for extra energy, brain food. Mom said fresh air was brain food, too. She was big on brain food. Eating a peanut butter/sprouts concoction was a good idea?

"Did you say 'Ma'am'?" Ms. Phillips muttered, checking her grade book brimming with school papers. "Wish I got this much respect from you during Language Arts class." Here's another script." Ms. Phillips pulled a dog eared copy from her educational debris. "Begin on page three, please."

What the heck is this? This is <u>not</u> the script I reviewed out in the darkened coat closet. "Page three? What's this? I mean, this is a little different from what I know. Uh, what I remembered." I corrected myself or Bumbling Bea did. We were beginning to muddle together and I couldn't keep us apart.

"A friend of mine at the university's drama department edited the old one and wanted to call it 'A Powhatan Powwow,' but it's still entitled 'John Smith and Pocahontas.' I told Principal Wells I wouldn't take on this project unless the script was edited." Ms. Phillips replied. "Did you know the other script was fifteen years old? What an antique. I'm surprised you kids don't know it by heart already. Well, Michiko would you read Pocahontas for me?"

The new girl slid in beside me on the stage. Her petite hands shook nervously as she spoke the lines. For a while she did a good job reading.

Even Bumbling Bea and I would admit it. But then the Michiko girl stumbled over a word like Bumbling Bea hoped she would.

"Relationship. The word is relationship not relatives," I corrected her.

"Thank you, Betty."

"Beatrice, not Betty." The hair on the back of my neck bristled at the new girl's mistake.

I *hated* the name Betty. Kids used it to tease me ever since preschool. But a long time ago, I created a good plan for this problem. Each year I wrote a report on my namesake Beatrice Mandelman, my mother's favorite abstract artist. She was awesome and after I showed the kids her artwork, they usually quit teasing me.

Ms. Phillips precariously perched herself on one of the dead grey chairs and suddenly noticed we stopped reading. Rubbing her forehead, she interrupted us. "Switch roles, please."

"Ms. Phillips, excuse me," the girl whispered. "I don't want to play John Smith. I want to play Pocahontas. I'm a girl. I can't play a boy's role. Well, I can but it would be so weird." Her teeny nose wrinkled.

I couldn't believe it. Michiko was insulted by Ms. Phillips request and showed it on her face. I tried not to smile or giggle, but inwardly I envisioned myself in front of the audience accepting bouquets of roses and signing autographs from my soon-to-be new best friends, the popular kids.

"Michiko, I understand you," explained Miss Phillips, "but you and Beatrice are the last students left here. Peter left right after his audition."

"He helps with his grandpa's lawn service and he's saving for a scooter," I added. *Always be helpful in an audition.* I repeated my actor's advice book's words over in my mind.

"Yes, 'Grandpa Fred's Lawn Service.' Peter shared with me about working to buy a scooter," answered Miss Phillips. "This is the way we do things here in our school, Michiko."

"Yes, Ms. Phillips, but you don't understand. I have to..." the girl looked panicked and blurted something I guessed was Japanese. Suddenly, Michiko stepped back and tripped over nearly all the folding chairs left standing. She escaped to the side exit door flying past the twins' jackets and blowing them to the floor. Like dominoes, the folding chairs metallic din shook the cinder block walls.

"Gee, what was all that about?" Bumbling Bea said.

"She's new, Beatrice," Ms. Phillips explained to me. "Obviously, she wants to be in this play."

Ms. Phillips was no fool. A ten year veteran teacher, she knew what most of her students thought—like a mind reader. Too bad I didn't have that talent.

"Gosh, Ms. Phillips, will you cast somebody who walks out of an audition? A good actress is one who respects authority, I thought." Bumbling Bea couldn't help saying it. A twinge of malicious guilt bubbled in my stomach. Feeling flushed, I stepped out of the left over mess of kid stuff I stood in and forced closed the chairs left standing.

I'm way more nervous than I have ever been. What's going on? I thought. Trying to look efficient to Ms. Phillips, I quickly collected the rubbish from the floor. My quick movements made me even more nauseous, but I couldn't give in now.

"So, you've read your father's book. *Acting Advice for the Anxious Actors,* isn't it? It was assigned reading when I took his class in college. I kept my copy. It was pretty helpful. Anyway, Beatrice, is there any other role you're interested in?" Ms. Phillips questioned.

A golden moment when all the planets aligned in my favor. I read about them in my father's book. Quote: "Make others see how well you fit the part. Distract them from your weaknesses."

I spoke carefully. "No, but I noticed you were still looking for a stage manager. You'll need some help with so many kids to watch over in the play, plus adding the fifth graders. How about Jerri? Or maybe the Michiko girl?"

Exhausted, Ms. Phillips slipped off her clogs and sat on a cardboard box full of basketballs. Writing notes on her clipboard, she answered, "Not a bad idea, but Jerri told me earlier all she wanted to be was a Pilgrim's wife. I think she can be of better use than a Pilgrim. And Michiko..."she stressed.

"Just wants to be Pocahontas," Bumbling Bea added snidely.

"Right," Ms. Phillips nodded as she gathered her things together. "So my decision is simple. I think I'll post the cast list this afternoon. Sure you don't want to read for another role? Your father mentioned at the parent committee meeting you showed an interest in working backstage."

I put the last chair away and brushed sneaker dust off the twins' jackets. When did I tell my dad I wanted to work backstage? Why did Ms. Phillips keep asking me that? Probably she was teasing me. I would be playing the starring role. Of course. I headed to the girls' restroom door and found Jerri slumped in a chair beside it.

"I couldn't do it," Jerri admitted flatly. "I got sick and barely made it here. I think the bite of your mom's Brain Food sandwich did it. Maybe I can draw play posters again this year."

We looked past each other thinking our own thoughts. I don't know what Jerri was thinking. I was thinking my usual thought: me decked out in a leather beaded Native American gown with leggings and moccasins crying *real* tears throughout my last dramatic speech.

Sighing at the same time, we heard the creak-swing-bang of the auditorium's double doors.

Ms. Phillips waved to us as she left the school building. "See you tomorrow, girls. I'm so excited for you."

"We're in? Let's go look at the cast list." Jerri whooped, zooming to the bulletin board in the front hallway.

"Bea, look. Ms. Phillips put me in anyway," Jerri marveled. "But where's your name?"

"I can't believe it. I can't believe it," I kept repeating.

I felt as sick as Jerri had, but I didn't make it to the bathroom door. I up-chucked my peanut butter and bean sprout sandwich right under the cast list.

Maybe it was a sign for me.

Chapter Three

Okay, I exaggerated a wee bit. I puked a little in the trash can which was below the cast list. I swear it was because of my weird sandwich at lunch and not nerves or I caught the flu going around school.

Anyway, there was a GINORMOUS cast list. I don't think Ms. Phillips turned down anyone who wanted to be in the show. Even our principal, Principal Wells, was in it. Ms. Phillips informed us she was including him. I didn't think she meant he would be *in* the show. I thought he would be backstage helping the kids on the stage crew.

"I am going to give Principal Wells a role in our show, too. He is around here all the time and this will give you a chance to know him better and vice versa. ("Vice Versa"? Who the heck uses the phrase "Vice Versa"? A Language Arts teacher, that's who.) All the students treat him as if he has some deadly disease. Heaven forbid he'd have any skills or talents. I know he's new to our school, but he's more than a disciplinarian. Apparently, he was quite the performer when he was in high school and college, so this year we're including him in our production," Ms. Phillips declared.

I snickered when Ms. Phillips announced this at the auditions. Principal Wells, an actor? You have got to be kidding me. I saw him after school hanging around the auditions flyer, but I thought he was taking a break from yelling at some delinquent kids. He may have some talents, though. I heard him singing when he supervised the hallway between classes. I don't know about acting, but he had a pretty good voice for an old guy.

Ms. Phillips was our new director for the play. Our old drama teacher, Mrs. Walker, retired from teaching after last year's show. Mrs. Walker was a nice lady, but nice was about all she had going for her. Like I said, she was nice and sometimes we students aren't so nice, you know? I guess she got tired of trying to inspire us to take the yearly play seriously.

When Mrs. Walker retired, someone had to become the drama teacher. Apparently, Ms. Phillips had a minor in Theater in college so it made her eligible to teach us. I'll say one thing for her - she sure knew how to organize things. Her room was the most organized classroom in school. I bet the messy stage drove her crazy during auditions.

"Look, Bea. Ms. Phillips gave Principal Wells a lead part. He's Powhatan, Pocahontas' father. Wow, she was serious about casting him." Jerri's voice was so soft, I could hardly hear her. "And look-- you're Michiko's rehearsal partner. You'll be super busy."

Huh? I knew I wasn't cast. I checked for my name by the role of Pocahontas right off the bat. The Michiko girl got the part. But rehearsal partner? What the heck?

"No, I'm the stage manager. I guess I pushed it too hard with Ms. Phillips. I've been doing that a lot lately and I don't know why. It's like someone has taken over my body and I'm only along for the ride. I figured this time since Ms. Phillips was the new director and knew my dad personally I'd have a shot at a big part. I barely know what a stage manager does let alone be someone's rehearsal partner."

Jerri looked over the rest of the cast list. "Oh my gosh, Peter is playing John Smith opposite Michiko. She's so tiny and he's so tall. What an odd combination. Gee, Bea. I thought you'd get Pocahontas for sure this year. There's only four eighth graders in the whole show—us, Peter and Michiko. We had zero competition this time," Jerri admitted.

She was right. No one above the sixth grade wanted to participate in the show and they didn't have to either, if they had performed in it once. By seventh grade, the regular kids had joined the soccer and basketball teams like they wanted to do all along. They got the required play thing out of the way as soon as they could.

My parents say, "Middle school is a tenuous (which means shaky) time in a youngster's life. Middle school students need a place to belong and explore various subjects in depth. Arts make for a civilized society. Since we both work in the arts, it only seems logical to us that you would love the arts, too."

My version: I attend Oak Grove Middle school because I had one choice—either go to this middle school which is close to my home or attend a normal one about eighteen million blocks away and too far to ride my bike which was my only form of transportation since my parents refused to drive me. I was lucky because I liked the arts. Lots of other kids weren't as lucky. They wanted to go to a normal school.

Well, I say normal because not the classes are centered on the arts in the other middle schools in town. Sometimes it's a little too much to understand. If we were truly an arts magnet school how come nobody wanted to be in the play? Even if the regular kids never played in a soccer game and sat on the bench the whole season it was better than being subjected to being in the yearly play more than once.

Nobody wanted to be in the play because the play was embarrassing times ten. No one learned their lines. You couldn't hear the actors past the front row and the costumes and sets were always pretty awful looking. Plus, we didn't have any money to make the show awesome. That was a big issue at school. The music department kept getting all the money for stuff they needed like choir risers and new band instruments and the dance squad got an awesome practice space. So the drama department was the last priority.

The play's budget consisted of borrowing stuff from the high school. We were stuck with their last year's set pieces and costumes if they would work for us. Last year they performed *You're a Good Man, Charlie Brown*—not exactly John Smith and Pocahontas material. You'd think someone would hold on to our costumes and set pieces each year, but they were always wretched looking and quickly dumped in the trash. It was easier to throw them away. We were in denial.

When I was in fourth grade I remembered seeing the annual show with my dad. It was a big deal to attend the middle school arts festivities. The choir concert, orchestra and band groups were awesome. Not the play. Even though the shows were pitiful, it was all the opportunity I would have in the near future to be involved in a play. This was the only play my school produced each year. When I was in sixth grade, my dad called old Mrs. Walker and asked her the reason for producing the same show each year. Her answer was, "This way, the students know the story of Pocahontas (our unofficial school mascot) and they will have a common language while they are students at Oak Grove."

My take on it? A common language? Did the teachers genuinely think we'd sit around at lunch and discuss, "Pocahontas was a strong willed woman," or "The story of John Smith and Pocahontas didn't occur as we have been told. Let's discuss it." Oh please. Weird, huh?

One year the kids wore poster board hats and plastic boot tops while the girls wore their mother's old skirts. Some brilliant parent suggested that the boys wear vests. That was the same year that the high school produced *Oliver* and scoured the town for vests for themselves. There were none to be found at the local thrift stores. So, Mrs. Gardner, our costume chairperson for the last ten years off and on (she had a lot of children go through Oak Grove Middle School) offered to create the vests herself out of "upcycled" grocery bags smelling faintly of vegetables and fruit. The boys hated them. They looked like they were back in kindergarten —poster paint symbols lined the front of the grocery bag with beads made out of construction paper dangling on the back in red and yellow yarn. Mrs. Gardner thought they were great and proudly mentioned them to my dad when we sat by her at the play. Plus, the production was held outside that year and the pathetic things wilted in the humid fall air and fell apart. The vests, I mean. The cast looked ridiculous and the audience giggled at them throughout the play.

Jerri slapped the cast list telling me, "Wait a minute. Ms. Phillips cast ten fifth graders in the show. They're extra pilgrims. And I'm in charge of them. She cast me as 'Kid Wrangler'..." Her voice trailed off as she plunked down sitting on her trumpet's case.

I wanted to laugh at Jerri, but how could I? Both of us were cheated that year. Only Peter and Michiko got a good deal. Well, Peter got a good deal. I didn't know if the Michiko girl understood what she was going to have to do as Pocahontas.

"This is my father's fault, you know. Last week, we went with him to his work's welcoming party for Michiko's father and he suggested the play to Michiko. I could scream at my father! He went on and on about the play. Michiko's dad wrote all the information on a napkin and tried to give it to her, but she was busy with her mom yelling at her. She'd worn a pair of cat ears to the party and her mom ripped them off of Michiko's head. It was embarrassing."

Twice before, I was introduced to Michiko. Parents do that. When they don't know what else to do they say, "Oh, my. You and So-and-So haven't met each other." You stand there and act like you have never seen the person before. You and the other person look more than awkward and embarrassed that A. your Mom (or Dad) doesn't remember introducing you to each other before and maybe they have early onset dementia or B. for some reason it's important for you to know So-and-So's name.

I said (well, it was Bumbling Bea who said it), "Okay, here's the plan. I know what I'm going to do ..."

I was interrupted by Principal Wells who appeared behind me, reading the cast list, too.

"Oh, good. That Michiko girl was terrific. I put my two cents in to Ms. Phillips about Michiko's talent, but I didn't think my opinion would matter much. Especially since Michiko is so shy." He talked to us like we didn't already know that about Michiko.

WHAT IS THE DEAL? Principal Wells gets to have an opinion about the casting?

"Congrats to you, Beatrice. And you, Jerri. I know you'll be great help to Ms. Phillips and the cast. See you tomorrow, fellow

Thespians," Principal Wells winked at us and took a little bow before he shuffled on down the hallway.

"I gotta go, Beatrice. We'll talk tomorrow, okay? But what was your plan?" Jerri asked.

"Never mind, Jerri. I gotta go, too. I'll tell you tomorrow after I refine it."

I always have a plan. Jerri was used to this. Most of my plans don't work—like the time I needed some money so I could go see *Wicked* for the fourth time. For three months, I collected soda cans. When I tried to return the eight garbage bags full of stinky, sticky things, I found out the grocery store no longer accepted them. What a rip-off.

But this was a much better plan than soda can collecting, even though I had only begun. First, I needed to go home and call my dear Dad the Professor.

Chapter Four

"Dad, you ripped me off! How could you?" I demanded yelling into the phone.

"Beautiful Beatrice, I don't know what you are talking about but by the fury I hear in your voice, I think you're about to tell me now."

My dad was a brilliant theater professor who taught at the university. He won all kinds of awards like Most Popular Professor which all the college kids voted on and some other awards from his colleagues (which I think is a funny word, don't you?) He wasn't always popular with me for the obvious "needing a break from the marriage" reason. And Dad meant well. He always told me so but sometimes he should KEEP QUIET.

"Why did you tell Mr. Tannabe about the school play auditions? Michiko auditioned and got the lead role!" I shouted in the phone.

"She did? Why, that's wonderful. What part are you playing?"

"Well, I'm not the lead role, am I? I'm the stupid stage manager and that Michiko girl's rehearsal partner. Whatever that is......." I mumbled.

"Stage manager? Terrific. I bet you'll get to do a bit of directing for your teacher. And also you'll be a rehearsal partner. My, your drama department is becoming serious about performing now, isn't it? "

Also, my dad was a certified looney. He thought the family needed to have a positive outlook all the time. All the time? He told me that when he was my age, he was always angry about things in his life until his younger brother died in a freak bicycling accident. From that day on, Dad decided that it was better to look at the bright side in any situation than to dwell on all the negatives in life. Seems to me that he hasn't looked for the bright side in his marriage....

My mother walked in from the kitchen as I threw my back-pack in the front hallway stairs. Mom was the most organized artist I had ever met. I thought artists were supposed to be extremely focused only on their art stuff? Whatever. Not my dear mother.

"Tossing your new back pack?" my mother stressed, whispering so Dad wouldn't hear. "Put away your things, Bea. We're having tofu casserole tonight."

That's another thing. My mother confused me. For instance, she drank diet soda but insisted on feeding us a Vegan diet. That's wrong. *Mom* ate Vegan. My brother and I ate around the perimeter of Mom's vegan thing—like snatching tidbits of pepperoni pizza at a friend's house or ordering huge steaks at a restaurant when Dad took us out eat. That sort of thing. We put up with it because we had no other choice. We tolerated a lot of things these days.

Last year after Dad moved out, Mom got on a raw food diet kick. One night, we were fed raw broccoli, raw cauliflower and raw carrots. My brother called it the "Irish Flag Dinner"—green, white and orange. Even though we don't eat that way anymore (thank goodness) my brother still titles our meals. I think his best was the "Cameroon Flag Dinner" which consisted of yellow zucchini, asparagus, beets and rice. I will admit these are some of his better jokes and we all have learned the colors of the world's flags whether we wanted to learn them or not.

I told my dad, "I will call you back later, okay? We have more to talk about." I hit the OFF button on the phone and turned to Mom. "Something was wrong with that sandwich, Mom. At the end of the auditions, I got sick and puked all over the place. No one eats bean sprouts and peanut butter."

"That's because it couldn't be called a PB & J. It would be called a PB & BS sandwich. The name is too long. Besides it sounds like you're eating peanut butter and poo," Edmund snorted at me as he skate boarded into the kitchen from the front porch.

"The sandwich didn't make you sick, Beatrice. It was because there's a flu going around. *You* didn't get a shot when you and Grandma Percy were at the drug store last week. If you recall, I suggested you get one this year since last year you were ill constantly. How did Jerri do? And Peter?"

My mother gently put in a dig about me not doing things her way nearly every day. "If you wore socks with your smelly canvas shoes, your feet wouldn't have gotten wet at the car wash when you begged to wash the car." Or "If you put away your clean laundry and not left it all over the floor, Bertie wouldn't poop in it." (It was Edmund's fault about my laundry. His dumb ferret got out of its cage.)

"If you recall Mother, Grandma P was in a big hurry to get home to watch the home shopping channel that day. She told me when she was a kid no one ever got flu shots." I loved correcting Mom.

"No one got shots when Grandma Percy was a child because then they didn't have flu shots. Ah, the wonders of modern medicine." Mom instructed as she slid the white and green casserole thing out of the oven. Yuck. White and green—it looked like mashed cottage cheese with seaweed. It probably was seaweed—"Nigerian Flag Dinner." Double yuck.

I called Dad right back and he answered the phone with, "Have a good attitude, Bea. No director wants to work with a pouty middle school girl."

I told you I was trying out being mean, right? Or rather, Bumbling Bea was trying it out. "Father-darling-happy face, will you *please* contact Ms. Philips and talk to her about Michiko playing the starring role. She can hardly speak English. Did you know that?"

"No."

"No, you didn't know that or no, you won't call Ms. Philips?" I queried.

"Both. Michiko's father told me that she has been reading and speaking English since she was eight years old. I think she's lovely. I know how much this meant to you, Beatrice but you told me that the person who plays Pocahontas becomes the most popular girl in school that year. That was your goal, right? To be popular? Can't you be popular without the part? You are such a great girl. I bet plenty of kids want to be your friend."

He was right about me saying the popular part. I did say I would like to be popular, but that's not *exactly* what I meant. I noticed whoever plays Pocahontas or John Smith was automatically invited to nearly all the boy/girl parties, birthday celebrations and sleep overs that the most popular eighth grade students' host. Of course the rest of the eighth graders wouldn't be caught dead in the play more than once themselves, but after the show was over it was a different matter. The entire school body talked about that year's Pocahontas and John Smith even if they were dreadful actors.

Popular kids had a special talent no one else noticed yet—they are fortune tellers. They can see the future for all of us.

"So-and-So is on her way to Broadway!" and "Hollywood, here comes So-and-So!" cheer the popular kids after the school play is over. Sometimes at football or basketball games or maybe a pep rally one of them will yell, "Number fifty-two (or whatever number the star player wore), to the NFL for you!" Or I'd hear one of the girls declare, "That Tiffany girl (or whatever cutesy name the star cheerleader was named) should be in 'Pump it Up.' She's as good a cheerleader as the (insert name of hot teen actress of the week) in that movie." I've discovered the popular kids kept close to the talented kids in case some of the talent might rub off on them.

"Not that many people want to be my friend." I stubbornly corrected him, "It's no big deal. You call Ms. Philips and tell her that, as her past professor that she loved so much *and* that this was the last time I could be in the show, surely she could recast the part with *me*," I suggested.

After saying aloud what was in my mind, I realized how ridiculous that sounded, but it was too embarrassing to take back without being more embarrassed, you know? I meant it would be nice to have a lot of friends--to do stuff with like get pedicures and sit with at lunch or maybe go see a movie? Looking ahead to high school which was in one more year, I saw Jerri and Peter as my only friends. They're great and all, but I've known them since we went to pre-school together. There wasn't much mystery between us anymore.

"Beatrice, your mother and I are not 'helicopter' parents," my dad informed me. "We don't swoop in when something goes wrong for our children. You've got to accept what life gives you even if it isn't fair in your eyes. This isn't earth shattering."

"A lot of life isn't fair," I wanted to say back to him and add, "like you left us and you're probably not coming back even though you haven't said so. Edmund and I didn't do anything wrong to deserve living without a father. That isn't exactly fair, now is it Dad?" But he didn't know that I felt that way.

"Yeah, a lot of life isn't fair," my dippy brother mimicked. "I didn't get too upset when Bernie got run over by that car on the same day my camping game website crashed. Remember?"

Edmund had built a camping game website and was so obsessed with it that he didn't notice "Bernie's Prison Break" as we now called it.

"Well, life's fair for you, bro'. Mom got you a new Bernie. Besides, it's your fault Bernie #1 escaped from his cage."

My Dad ended the argument with, "Beatrice, I won't call Ms. Philips and neither will your mother. If you don't want to be in the play, quit. You've earned enough outside arts credits to go on the yearly trip at this point anyway. Hopefully, you'll make the trip this year since you've missed the other two years."

It was true. I had all the outside arts credits I needed. See, since we're an arts integration school we students had an opportunity to travel together to New York City over spring break. But we could only travel one time while we're in middle school because there were so many of us. I've missed the trip the last two years because my great aunt passed away two days before the first trip time and I had to have my tonsils taken out the next year since they were way gross and infected.

The deal was that students must be involved in one play, one choir and one art class over the course of their middle school career. All the students loved choir, orchestra, band and art. We sang and played different music all the time and the art teacher was plain cool. Jerri had been playing trumpet since she was in sixth grade and absolutely loved it. Peter was the best boy singer in choir. I held the clarinet and pretended to play and I'm not much of a singer. Theater was my only hope. So, I figured if I kept at it, I'd get good at it. Plus, Dad would be proud of me if I won the lead role this year and I'd take the trip to NYC I missed the last two years.

Now my hopes were ruined by a cat ears wearing new girl from Japan.

I chewed and chewed the spongy tofu in the casserole. Horrible.

"Okay, fine. I'll smile, help, organize, rehearse the Michiko girl and maybe get to direct with Ms. Philips." I smiled with a little smirk.

"And?" Dad asked dramatically.

"And I'll enjoy it, Father Dear," I lied as dramatically and hung up the phone. Touché.

That's what he thinks, I thought. My plan was in motion. I wasn't ready to share it with anyone.

Chapter Five

My plan was working and I had to thank that Michiko girl. She gets all the credit.

Rehearsals began promptly after school at 3:30 p.m. School was over at 3:15 p.m. That gave the cast a chance to get their stuff out of their lockers, have a snack and talk crazy fast with their friends.

The rule was that the auditorium's doors lock at 3:30, so if a kid moves too slowly or walks to Herman's Ice Cream Bar and doesn't make it back on time, he was locked out. Once you're locked out three times, you are cut from the play and you have to wait a whole year to be in the next play and maybe get to go to New York during spring break. Personally, I think this is a bit like prison, but there are lots of other times that school feels like prison anyway so what's the use in fighting it?

There was one way to save yourself if you are late to rehearsal, but you have to know the secret. You had to have a buddy waiting inside the auditorium to sneak you through the boiler room door that led outside. Most of the time there was at least one moment at the beginning of rehearsal when the director wasn't watching the cast. I've only snuck in once and Jerri let me inside. Peter was too much of a chicken to be late to rehearsal because he said that it made him nervous all day just thinking about it.

Anyway, it was 3:29 and Michiko still hadn't arrived at rehearsal. Ms. Philips' first job for me was to take role.

This is awesome. Michiko is going to be locked out and maybe I would get to play Pocahontas after all instead of the boring job of taking roll. Ugh, I thought.

There were so many Olivias, Tatums, Zoeys, Haileys and Hunters that I needed to take roll before the doors locked. I wanted to be efficient and have us ready to go as soon as possible. Already I saw that Ms. Philips needed a better method of taking roll because calling all the names took forever.

The doors locked as planned. Ms. Philips explained the attendance policy, rehearsal calendar and answered questions. There weren't many but I'm sure lots of kids will stop Ms. Philips and ask the same question over and over afterward. Usually, the kids are more interested in reading the script and seeing how many lines they have than to listen another five minutes to a teacher.

I looked around for Michiko again. This was great. This was fabulous! Michiko was nowhere to be seen.

STRIKE NUMBER ONE.

"Ms. Philips, everyone is here today, but one of the Olivias. One of the Haileys told me she went home early with that yucky flu." I spoke slowly and stressed, "Also, *Michiko* isn't here, but she was present at school today. I guess she's *late*. What do you want me to do?"

I was interrupted by someone tapping me on my shoulder. Darn. It was Michiko.

"Betty, your friend Jerri let me in the door. I'm sorry I'm late, Ms. Philips."

WHAT? Jerri saved Michiko?

"That's all right, Michiko. I wish the doors didn't automatically lock at 3:30, but it can't be changed. I asked Principal Wells about it to see if it could be altered but it's not possible. Make sure you are on time tomorrow, Michiko."

"Yes ma'am. I apologize. That's a wonderful outfit, Bett-- I mean Beatrice. Did you create it?"

Okay, enough! First, she calls me "Betty" which I corrected her about at the auditions. Secondly, she and Jerri were friends? That's news to me. Third, Ms. Philips didn't even get angry with her. Last year's teacher/director Mrs. Walker would have screamed at her. She screamed a lot.

And Michiko was making fun of my outfit. Bumbling Bea picked it out and she thought it was rockin'. I had on a short pink skirt with two different knee socks (one was striped and one was hearts, a gift left over from Valentine's day), a shirt from fifth grade that was too little but looked super cool over a tank top that peeked out at the straps and high top basketball shoes I had found at the thrift store. Plus, I had seen a photograph of my mom in 1982 and her hair was pulled up into a side ponytail. I'd done that, too. Kids looked me over that day, but I knew it was because they wished they looked the same way. I didn't know why they were snickering at me so much. Nobody snickered at Michiko in her cat ears and she wore them all the time.

After Ms. Philips gave us cast notes which she said would happen before each rehearsal, we handed out the scripts and began to read. At the first rehearsal we always sit in a circle and read the script aloud. This is fun for the kids playing main characters, but pretty boring for the kids with no lines. I looked over at Jerri and she was trying to play Duck Duck Goose with the fifth graders, but they were already disinterested. I drew the New York skyline on my script. "Keep your eyes on the goal" my Dad's acting book coached.

Miss Phillips spent a lot of time roaming around the group pointing out where we were in the script, nodding her head and chewing on her pencil. The only person who seemed to know what was going on was that Michiko girl. It's because she was nervous about her big part. I'm beginning to think that Ms. Phillips cast Michiko because she felt sorry for her.

Here came STRIKE TWO.

Michiko slapped her script and blurted, "Ms. Phillips this script is inaccurate. This is a mistake. Pocahontas did not wear any clothes. When John Smith met her, she was naked."

The whole cast burst out in fits of laughter. The fifth graders were no longer bored and several turned bright red in the face. Peter's eyes were about the size of a Frisbee when he choked out, "What?"

Ms. Phillips shushed the cast. "Yes, I know, Michiko. But I don't think that would go over well in a middle school play. Sometimes we have to bend the facts of history a little to make theatre friendly and acceptable to the public."

I heard Peter mutter, "Oh, man. That was close for a second."

But Michiko persisted. "Ms. Phillips, in the Greek theater, for example, their plays included characters whose eyes were gouged out and whole villages were put into slavery. Children were stolen away from their parents. The Greeks told gruesome tales. We must honor the Greeks by telling our story factually. If we don't tell the story of Pocahontas and John Smith factually, it is like we never told the story at all."

This stumped Ms. Phillips, but she was such a smart teacher she quickly answered. "That's true, Michiko but we only read the Greek plays in Language Arts class and we don't present them for the public. Cast, how do you feel about Pocahontas dressed as though she's naked. Her costume could be flesh colored?"

Principal Wells looked like he was wary of where this conversation was going and was about to step in, when someone said, giggling, "Wouldn't that be distracting and kinda' weird? If it looked like Pocahontas was naked?"

So, we voted and of course, Ms. Phillips won and we went back to Pocahontas wearing her usual costume and not looking naked. Whew.

After about twenty more minutes when rehearsal was about to wrap up, Michiko stood quickly declaring, "This isn't right, Ms. Phillips. I will concede (What eighth grader uses the word 'concede'?) on the nudity of Pocahontas debate, but I can not tolerate the ending of the play. Pocahontas did not stand in front of John Smith and beg for his life. She...she..."

Quickly and dramatically, Michiko stood tossing her beloved cat ears to one of the Tiffanys, grabbed her chair abruptly and dragged Peter to the center of the circle of cast members and draped him over her chair. It went like this. "Please Father, I love Smith. I must be with him!"

Michiko stopped. She froze with her eyes crossed and opened them wide, her skinny Minnie Mouse arms poised in the air. Her face was twisted and contorted, like she was angry or something. Her head and arms shook ever so slightly, like a little shiver but in a frozen position.

Ms. Phillips stood and looked concerned.

Principal Wells stood and looked flabbergasted.

We all stood, looked at her and then each other and back at her.

"Oh my gosh, Michiko? Is something wrong?" Jerri asked.

Silence.

Huh? What the heck was that?

I looked at Ms. Phillips. "Should I get the nurse? She's still here." I didn't wait for an answer from Ms. Phillips. I jogged slowly to the auditorium door when Michiko recovered or unfroze or something.

"What did you think, Ms. Phillips? I struck a mie pose from Kabuki Theater. It's pronounced mee-eh." She stood proudly and continued lecturing us. "It's used in an ancient type of theater in Japan that is one of our most famous Japanese assets. I want to be a Kabuki actor when I grow up, but only males are allowed to be them. I thought the pose would be affective to use in the play." Michiko smiled.

Ms. Phillips stammered, "Yes, it certainly was effective. We were all stunned. Weren't we, Principal Wells?"

Principal Wells retrieved Peter from his prostrate position on the chair. He looked freaked out, but then so did Principal Wells in a grownup sort of way. "Well, Michiko. You sure had us going there for a moment. Kabuki Theater, huh?" Principal Wells chuckled.

Great! Principal Wells was even more impressed with Michiko. I thought I might as well quit the show while I could. Pretty soon Ms. Phillips was going to talk to me about the rehearsal partner thing with Michiko--if not today, then tomorrow. How could I wrestle the Pocahontas part away from the Michiko girl if the entire world loved her?

"All right cast, that's enough for today. We'll begin blocking the first few pages tomorrow. Make sure you have your scripts and...?" Ms. Phillips coaxed.

"Pencils!" the cast yelled back to her.

"Yes! Beatrice I need to speak to you for a moment. Please wait, will you? Michiko, you, too," Ms. Phillips called as she wrestled herself out of the pack of fifth graders who were descending upon her like the paparazzi over some celebrity. It takes a long time for fifteen elementary kids to say good-bye to a teacher. If one person gets a bit more "hugging time" (like four seconds) with the teacher, the hugging line begins all over again. Poor Ms. Phillips. I bet she thought her idea of including them was a bit premature. Yes, I say 'premature.' I can use big words like Michiko.

"So, girls we need to talk about the rehearsal partnering between you. Do you think you can get along with each other well enough to work together? I've noticed some simmering hostility between you." Boy, that Ms. Phillips. She saw a lot more of what is going on than I thought.

"I have no problems with Michiko." Then Bumbling Bea appeared before I could stop her. "But she was late to rehearsal and she interrupted you twice." I looked over my nose at Michiko turning my head to her ever so regally. "As stage manager it's my job to help keep the rehearsals moving along smoothly. We take this seriously here at our school. I don't know about what you do in Japan at your school, but..."

Michiko stared at me. Her huge black eyes filled with tears. "I was trying to... trying to be helpful. I was excited about this play because I thought it would give me an opportunity to use..." she muttered. Before I knew it, she grabbed her pink backpack and violin case and rushed out of the auditorium, the doors slamming behind her.

"Well, that's great," Ms. Phillips said sarcastically.

STRIKE THREE?...

I recoiled from my last statement to Michiko and was able to control Bumbling Bea who disappeared as quickly as she arrived. "I'm sorry, Ms. Phillips. I was trying to be helpful." I realized I accidentally mocked Michiko by using her same words in the same tone. Have you ever done that? Bumbling Bea was jealous of Michiko and she was digging me into a hole more and more.

Remember I told you that I planned to wrestle Michiko's part away from her? Even though my plan wasn't working as I hoped, it was still working. I was keeping my sights on my goal like my dad's book advised. Now, I needed to have a chance to talk with Peter and ask him for his help. He would be the game changer.

Chapter Six

On the way out of school after rehearsal, I caught up with Peter. He was always in a hurry to get home and put in a little time helping his grandpa. Even though Jerri and I considered ourselves as BFFs, I was a better best friend to Peter.

"Hey, Beatrice. Whatcha' think of that thing Michiko did? Pretty cool, huh?"

Peter's legs were so long, I could hardly keep up with him. "What? Oh yeah. Interesting and weird," I said, changing the subject. "I wanted to talk to you about something, Peter."

"Okay, but hurry. I gotta get home and help Poppa rake leaves."

Wow. My strategy was lining up so easily. I whispered to Peter, "Would you like to make an easy fifty dollars? How close are you to your goal to buy that scooter?"

"I'm half way there." Peter informed me proudly. "So, what's the deal?"

This was one of those times that happen about once a year in your beige life, you know? When what you'd been thinking about, dreaming about, happens and life gets a lot more colorful. I stopped jogging to keep up with him and coyly offered, "I'll pay you fifty dollars to sabotage Michiko's performance in the play." Bumbling Bea raised her head to finish with, "And I'll even throw in another five if it keeps her entirely out of the play." I don't know where that came from. "Throw in"? I sounded like a gangster in some old black and white movie Dad watched over and over again.

That worked. I had his attention.

"Like what? Don't wear deodorant for a couple of days so when I stand by her it'll fumigate her?" He laughed. "That's a pretty good one. I used it last summer when I was in summer choir camp and had to stand in the tenor section by that dweeb Lance Klink who kept bugging me. Man, he found out the hard way when I raised my arms and waved my arm pits toward him. I was serious about him getting outta' of my face..."

"How about...how about doing something with poison ivy? You said your grandpa told you about how he wasn't allergic to poison ivy and you probably weren't, either." I was hoping he'd come up with his own idea. Mine was kinda' feeble.

"Oh, yeah. He said lots of people aren't allergic to poison ivy. He wasn't, so I wasn't allergic because it's genetic or something. That's why I could help rake it out of Mrs. Pierson's back yard. Boy, she had an entire crop growing back there." Peter began walking fast again.

46

I grabbed for the jacket on his back, stopping him. "You're the smart guy, P. Can't you think of something to do with it that would annoy Michiko? I don't know, like wave it in her face, so she screams and Ms. Phillips scolds her (my mind was racing now) and Michiko will cry hysterically and dash off the stage and quit the show. Ms. Phillips would have to give the part to me. That's my plan. Just once I want to play Pocahontas in this crummy play!"

"You're begging? You must be desperate. What's with you and all this plan stuff anyway? You have more plans than Congress." Peter punched my arm.

"P.!" Bumbling Bea was frantic. "How's about it? (How's about it? Did I say that?) I'll pay you fifty dollars and tip..."

"Ten dollar tip," he interrupted.

"Fine. You win. I'll tip you ten dollars if it works. That's all the money I have, so don't mess up. You'll do it at tomorrow's rehearsal?"

By the time I'd made the deal with Peter, we were near our houses. As P. left me he yelled, "Sure, cool! Whatever. See ya!"

I stood there on the sidewalk and threatened aloud, "He better not mess this up."

I was relieved about one thing. It occurred to me that Peter and I didn't agree on how much I'd pay him if the poison ivy thing *didn't* work. I learned that lesson the hard way, when I promised Grandma Percy that I'd take care of her plants while she was on vacation in Florida and I drowned them in plant food. Grandma said she wouldn't pay me because I killed her prized orchids... even though I did the job.

I was so excited. I would be playing the lead part and the popular kids would know it. Like I said, popular kids know the future way ahead of everyone else. I think that's part of the reason they are popular.

I thought, *Peter is a brainiac. He'll come up with something great.*

I felt itchy merely thinking about our plan and sped home singing badly all the way. My plan was working out. I stopped on the sidewalk leading to our house, let out a Michael Jackson hoot, took one big leap skipping all three steps and landed on the front porch of our house.

Not bad.

Chapter Seven

As So and So, the famous writer, wrote in the *Tale of Two Cities*, "It was the best of times, it was the worst of times." I had never read the book that quote came from, but I felt the best and worse when Peter and I tried to sabotage Michiko's rehearsal and tried to get her to quit the show. It seemed so simple: When Ms. Phillips wasn't looking, Peter would wave some poison ivy in front of Michiko, and she'd scream, make a scene, and quit the show. Simple revenge on my part or so I thought.

"The Sabotage of Michiko" day was fabulous. I aced my Spanish test, been one of the first kids in line for lunch (chicken nuggets), ran the mile in P.E. in less than nine minutes (which was unbeliev- able for me) and mustered the courage to say hi to the new boy in science class. His name was Bronson and he had dark wavy hair, a quirky smile, blue eyes, and a great laugh that made you feel like the joke you told him was funny even if you thought it was stupid. And he lives one block away from me. (Am I gushing? Sorry.)

Bronson was the first boy to ever say hi to me before I said hi to him. I put him on top of the "cute new boy" list. I desperately prayed that no one notices Bronson or if they do and he notices them, he'll still think my jokes are the most funny.

It was a favoloso (that's Italian for fabulous) day until rehearsal time. Feeling pretty cool, I sashayed my way to the door of the auditorium seven minutes ahead of time and walked into an all-out war between the fifth grade boys and the sixth grade girls. The yelling boys were chasing the screaming girls around the auditorium with pretend boogers on their fingers yelling, "Wanna see my brain innards?"

I brought a whistle that I planned to use for crowd control and gave it a loud tweak. The boys stopped running and the girls faked a sigh of breathy exasperation. *Not a bad technique. I feel like a basketball coach.* I thought. I took roll and noticed that several of the students were absent. There were rumors of a nasty, long lasting flu hovering around school that picked off students one by one.

Peter was nowhere to been seen. Remember, he was always early to rehearsals because he was afraid he'd be locked out. So, where was he?

"Anybody seen Peter? He was here at lunch," I questioned the cast.

"I saw him in the nurse's office. He didn't look so good. Maybe it's the flu thing!" Jerri called as she corralled the booger boys.

Michiko decided to give her help. Sheesh. "I talked to him at lunch and he said that he was itchy all over and thought he got a rash from the walnuts he ate last night at dinner."

Walnuts at dinner? I'd known Peter for nearly all my life and he had no allergies. Once he said he was allergic to math, but who wasn't?

I turned to see Michiko who was wearing a bandana over her head. "You can't wear hats or bandanas in school, except on crazy hat day. School policy," I informed her.

"Yes, I am aware of that. My mother made me memorize the school handbook when I moved here. There's a reason I'm wearing it, though. Where is Ms. Phillips?" Michiko turned away from me. Seeing Ms. Phillips, she skipped quickly to the edge of the stage and called, "Ms. Phillips. I have another idea for my character. I think you'll like it very much!"

"How about after rehearsal we talk about it, Michiko?" Ms. Phillips suggested as she hurried on to the stage. "Cast, I'm sorry I'm late—short faculty meeting about tomorrow's field trip. Let's begin on page one of the script, shall we? Please take the places listed in the stage directions. At the top of the page?" She pointed. "It says, 'John Smith's party is grouped up center.'"

Still no Peter. Where the heck was he? As Ms. Phillips walked over to the John Smith party to fix their positions into a "pretty stage picture," there was a loud knocking --more like a banging-- at the auditorium door.

Jerri called back. "I think it's Peter." She looked embarrassed, but confident (if that's possible). "I know his knock," she stammered.

Did Jerri know something I didn't?

"Well, let him in Jerri. We can't exactly rehearse the show without Pete..." Ms. Phillips stopped abruptly.

Jerri opened the door for Peter. He walked judiciously to the front of the stage. His head was lowered, but I noticed a bunch of chalky looking pink spots painted like giant dots across his neck.

"Are you okay, Peter? We were talking about you."

He quietly mumbled, "Sure. Ms. Phillips. I'm okay." He turned to all of us on the stage demanding, "What's the big deal, anyway? Quit staring!"

OH. MY. GOSH.

Peter drifted on to the stage near me, scratching his arm so hard welts appeared making faint pink stripes running down to his wrist. I noticed little raised bumps ran down his neck. At one point, they stopped and leapt toward the opening of his tee shirt which Peter kept pulling away from his neck at the same time he was striping his arm with his scratching. He was very busy. I'm no authority, but I think that's an allergic reaction to something... Like an allergic reaction to poison ivy? But Peter said his grandpa told him he probably wasn't allergic to it. *Probably...*

Oops.

Peter took his place on stage in front of his group. Michiko stared at him quizzically. Or at least I think it was quizzically. I had my head down for most of the next part, because I was pretty sure the polka- dotted- Peter problem was entirely my fault.

"Mr. Smith, welcome to our village. I am Pocahontas, Powhatan's daughter. Please come and sit here." Michiko gestured to stage left. She explained to me directly, "I know the script says that I take Peter down stage right, but stage left is a much better position."

"You can't do whatever you want to, Michiko. You have to follow the script and it says to cross down right. Jeez." I mumbled to myself.

I heard a rustling and a gasp from the kids behind Peter and Ms. Phillips. Suddenly Peter whisked off his tee shirt and abruptly threw it to the ground at my feet. There he was in all his glory. Peter didn't have dots only on his neck. He was covered in welts all over his chest and back, too. It must have itched something fierce, because he stood with his arms out from himself, like a rag doll. Well, a boy rag doll. A rag doll boy? Obviously, I was pretty freaked by what I saw standing there in front of me. I tried not to giggle, but I did anyway. Bumbling Bea struck again...

"Peter. What happened to you? You were fine this morning in class. Did you eat something you're allergic to?" Ms. Phillips looked worried.

Peter leered at me. "No, Ms. Phillips. These are welts from poison ivy touching my skin. Unbeknownst to me, I'm allergic to it!"

Some of the fifth grade boys snickered at Peter's comment, but Michiko stepped down center and exclaimed, "Oh that's terrible, Peter. I'm fortunate. I am not allergic to anything."

I give Michiko credit. I think she realized that wasn't the right thing to say at the moment and quietly moved over by Ms. Phillips.

"Ms. Phillips, do you want me to stand in for Peter? He could just watch the rehearsal," I suggested.

"Yes, I guess so Beatrice. I don't think we have much of a choice, do we?" Ms. Phillips said sighing.

At that moment, Peter jumped off the stage (which is a BIG no-no) and gently deposited himself into a front row seat ever so carefully, trying not to touch the arm rests on either side of him. He twitched and wiggled uncontrollably like you do when you have an itch in the middle of your back and you can't reach it (that always drives me crazy). Seeing this, all the prissy seventh grade girls sitting near him quickly moved away as if they could get infected by breathing his air.

As I took Peter's place on the stage, there was another rustling and gasp from the cast and Ms. Phillips. Michiko dramatically whisked off the scarf on her head and stood smiling happily. There on top of her usual pretty blue black hair was a thin plastic cap. I think it's used by hairstylists to hi-light hair. My mom's had her hair done that way before. It was jammed all the way down on to her forehead. A few wisps of her hair had slipped out and around the cap. She looked like a sea urchin, an anemone to be exact.

"Pocahontas was bald when she met John Smith. The children's heads were shaved because of lice. Well, what do you think?" Michiko proudly puffed out her chest.

"Bald *and* naked! How absolutely embarrassing..." I chirped.

"And gross," someone added. Lots of kids snickered at that remark.

"Cast, quiet please. Michiko, this must be what you wanted to speak to me about, right?" Ms. Phillips sounded a little angry. She took a big gulp of her diet cola. "You've disrupted the rehearsal, Michiko. Please put on your scarf and we'll talk about this later."

This was great. FINALLY! Ms. Phillips took care of the Michiko problem for me without my even having to step in myself. Oh, yeah...

Ms. Phillips again sighed loudly saying, "Since this rehearsal is a bust, I think it would be best if we played some drama games for the rest of the time. Michiko and Beatrice, I want you to go out in the hallway and practice Michiko's part together."

Bumbling Bea appeared out of nowhere. I hadn't figured on my alter ego showing up right at that moment but as I have mentioned before I can't control her. "I can't, Ms. Phillips," I stammered, "I have to go home early today. My dad is coming over today."

There was no way I would help Michiko with her part. Well, Bumbling Bea wasn't going to help Michiko. We were too far into the lie to back out now. Michiko drove me crazy! I was sick of her attitude and bizarre costuming ideas. I couldn't take another minute of it. I guess Michiko knew this about me, because before I could say anything else she had grabbed her violin and backpack and sprinted for the door.

Except she dropped something.

A note.

I jammed Bumbling Bea back down in my throat. It's one thing to be mean to someone when no one is there to see it happen, but it's another thing when the whole world is watching. "Hey, Michiko you dropped something..." I called but it was too late. She zipped out the auditorium door as quickly as she talks.

Maybe it's an important assignment or something, I said to myself.

What a bunch of baloney. I was kidding myself.

I opened it. It was a copy of an email note. The note was written in some other language than English. I decided it was probably Japanese. With the note was a photo of an actor costumed in a red kimono and white woman's wig with black chopsticks looking things poking out from its head. His face (her face?) was scary looking—all white with black markings. His mouth was wide open and his eyes crossed like he wanted to freak you out. It worked on me.

"Whoa, what is this photo? And more important, why does Michiko have it?" I mumbled to myself. I quickly jammed the note in my back pocket and slipped out the auditorium doors.

Michiko was mysterious. I never figured on that.

Chapter Eight

As I left school and headed for the bike rack, I watched Michiko galumph down the side walk with her oversized pink backpack and violin case. I was pretty impressed at her agility despite all the extra weight.

"Whatcha' do that for, Beatrice? What's up with you?" Jerri asked as she stepped out the front door hallway letting the heavy door slam behind her.

"What? I thought we were stopping rehearsal since Michiko modeled her little hairdo and you were playing drama games instead or something?" I rearrange my script nonchalantly.

"Ms. Phillips gave up on the games and cancelled the rest of rehearsal because the kids were getting squirrelly. Now she's freaked because we're behind. Tomorrow's the field trip to the art museum and to see the play, you know. She doesn't think we'll catch up in time before next week's performance."

Jerri flipped the combination lock quickly and yanked her bike off the rack. We'd ridden our bikes to school each year since we learned to ride. We felt independent that way. "You lied to Ms. Phillips. You told her you needed to get home early. You didn't want to help Michiko with her part. It is so obvious you don't like her." Jerri slammed her backpack on the ground throwing her math textbook on top of it.

I thought about Michiko. Did she know I didn't like her? Did she know I was trying to get out of helping her? Did I honestly care whether she knew I didn't like her? She looked so ridiculous standing there in that wig cap thing with her hair shooting out of its pores. Bald, my butt.

"I don't know what you're talking about. Michiko interrupted rehearsal, not me." I mocked her, "'Oh, look cast. I'm a bald Pocahontas.' Bald, my butt." I snorted and looked at Jerri to see if she was laughing, too. She wasn't. "Erenajay, what did I do that was so bad?" Sometimes, we spoke in pig Latin since we learned it in third grade. It was a sort of a secret language Jerri and I used when we wanted to get each other's attention.

Along came Peter. He gave me a mean look and I knew I had to fix what I had begun. "Here, Peter. Here's the fifty dollars I promised you." I respectfully tried to put the money in his pocket but he quickly threw it at me like it was lit on fire.

"No thanks. I don't want your stupid money. It's all your fault I have poison ivy over my entire body." He was scratching his inner thigh and winced when he took a step. "I can't even carry my backpack. Much less ride my idiot bike that *could* be a scooter *someday*."

"Here, give me your back pack. I'll carry it for you. It's the least I can do..." I trailed off.

"Didn't you hear me? I don't want your money or your help or anything to do with you. Your plan didn't work. Of course, they never do. I'm miserable because of you!" Peter yelled at me.

"What are you talking about, Peter?" Jerri asked. "What plan?"

"Ask her," Peter huffed.

I looked at Jerri. "It's Bumbling Bea's fault, not mine." That sounded so dumb. Who was I kidding? "Oh, never mind. I mean, it's my fault. I promised to pay Peter fifty dollars if he'd wave some poison ivy in Michiko's face and cause a scene. It sounded like a good plan at the time..."

"What's the deal with you and Michiko anyway? You told Ms. Phillips you would take any part. That means you would accept any role she gave you, even if it was working backstage. You're a phony..." Jerri bicycled away from me adding, "...and cruel." She stopped at the corner of the street and yelled back, "And don't call me Erenajay. Pig Latin is lame. I'm not sure I want to be friends with you anymore. Lately, I feel like I don't even know you."

Peter hadn't abandoned me yet but looked at me square on, "Yeah, Jerri's right. You've gotten so mean. Michiko is a nice person. All you do is try to hurt her feelings to get her to quit the show. Jeez, it's not like this is Broadway or something." He hoisted his pack over the handlebars of his bike like a ship's figurehead.

I knew they were right. I didn't even recognize myself. I mean, I looked pretty much the same except for scary bands of pimples that kept popping up on my forehead. But man, I felt different on the inside. Was Bumbling Bea taking me over?

I looked at my bike and looked at my friends, "I wanted to be a big deal--just once in school. No one even notices I'm alive and Dad has practically abandoned me. Next year, we're in high school and..." I turned to Peter, but he didn't hear me. He had already pedaled off and was slowly catching up with Jerri.

I walked my bike home and left it outside by the azalea bushes near the front porch. In the back pocket of my jeans, I still had the copy of Michiko's email and the weird looking photo of that old Japanese guy.

I headed into the house missing Edmund's skateboard that was blocking the stairs. Edmund skipped down the stairs three at a time and jumped right in front of me barely missing the skateboard.

"You moron, Edmund. Can't you see your skateboard is in my way? It's a safety hazard." I squinted my eyes at him.

"What's bugging you? I leave it there all the time and you've never once complained." Edmund balanced the board on his head while he slobbered all over a cow-lick-sized jaw breaker. It was so big; his mouth didn't even fit around it. Consequently he drooled all over his shirt. It was pretty gross.

"Nothing. Sorry I called you a moron. I'm going to my room, so don't bother me." I added, "I'm gonna do some research on the laptop, so don't come barging in my room and want it because it's my day for it, you know?" We shared Dad's old lap top. It was super old, but it still sort of worked for things like doing research on the internet and playing games which is about all we needed it for.

By the time I apologized to Edmund he didn't even hear me. He was on his way to the kitchen to put away his jawbreaker for another day. Yes, he kept them around in an old pickle jar. Again—gross!

I turned on the laptop, opened my bedroom window to catch the cool fall breeze and waited for the ancient thing to boot up. Finally, after I had gone to get a snack (raisins, my favorite), the computer clicked on after a bunch of buzzing, dinging and some strange lady's velvety voice advertising, "Hello, you're on the internet." I told you it was an antique.

I typed in, "Kabuki Theater" and in came a bunch of entries for it. There were loads of sites to pick from: Japan4u.com, Japanland.com, and Japandream.com were a few. I've always been fascinated by website names. Who thinks them up? Well, anyway, I randomly picked one that looked good enough to help me. It stated Kabuki Theater was an ancient type of theater dating back to the seventeenth century that's performed by men only. Then there was the interesting part. The women were the first performers but it was considered inappropriate for them to perform for the public so the men took it over. *Figures that men would hog it*, I thought. I skipped some boring parts and read on...

It's considered:

melodramatic, like soap operas

some plays were based on folk tales

the language was old sounding and hard to understand and follow the plays were acted on a large, revolving stage

stage left was for important or high-ranking characters

stage right was occupied by lower-ranking characters

actors performed "kata" which were certain types of movement

the kata have been performed exactly the same for many generations

a "mie" was one type of kata where the actor's eyes crossed and exaggerated an expression

"Aha!" I cheered. "Now I'm getting somewhere. That mie pose was what Michiko did at the rehearsal a few days ago. It's all making sense to me now." But the photo? Who was that in it? Did Michiko get some photo from a fan website or did she know him?

I turned the photo over. There was a handwritten note on the back of it. Written in Japanese I thought.

私はあなたを見て非常に興奮しています！

敬具

叔父

"Great. Another stumbling block in this whole charade," I mumbled. I put the note and photo in the outside pocket of my backpack for safe keeping.

Edmund appeared at my door, "Mom said to tell you it's time for dinner. Oh, and Michiko is on the phone for you."

What? Why was Michiko calling me? Did her mother make her call me to apologize or was she expecting me to apologize? Or did she want to pick a fight?

"Left overs? Is it the Nigerian flag dinner? Ugh. Beat you there!" I taunted, but Edmund was out the door sliding down the backstairs on his butt singing some stupid rap song about boogers. Boys.

Chapter Nine

I couldn't believe I agreed to it. I was Michiko's bus partner on the field trip! I blamed the next whole calamity on my mom instead of my dad this time, although he was still on my short list of people I was mad at. Mrs. Tannabe had Michiko call our house and ask if my mom could chaperone the field trip for her.

"Poor Mrs. Tannabe has a migraine," Mom lamented.

My mother was a wonderful person. I was being sarcastic. My mom is always a wonderful person. She quickly came to Mrs. Tannabe's rescue and agreed to help her out.

Oh joy...

Michiko was going to be field trip partners with her mother because she didn't think she had any friends. My dear mother suggested that Michiko ask me. Wouldn't that be more fun? What could Michiko say? What could I say? Once Michiko spoke with

Mom, she put me on the line to talk to that Michiko girl and I was trapped.

I might as well have be Michiko's partner. I deserved her. Jerri wouldn't talk to me and Peter was mad at me because of the poison ivy thing. I was alone. Things in my life were getting worse instead of better.

They say keep your friends close, but keep your enemies closer. Seated by each other on a Yellow Dog (that's a loving name for a school bus if you didn't know) was about as close as two enemies like Michiko and I could get. Even with the bus windows wide open the ride was excruciating. The bus air was stinky and moist like unwashed hair and sweaty tennis shoes, and the kids behind us talked and sang way too loud. The ride didn't seem to bother them. Any field trip was exciting. How could they have so much fun when I was miserable?

Thankfully, I wasn't a member of the Bus Butt Crew. You know, those are the kids that ride a school bus to school each day, year after year? Also, I forgot the ins and outs of school bus etiquette since the last time I'd gone on a field trip, so I ended up sitting up front with Michiko right behind mom. Some of the popular kids snickered when I sat behind my mother. Even if you love your mom a whole lot and would do about anything for her, you aren't supposed to sit near her on the bus. It's not cool. You look like a little kid and who wants to be that?

When the bus hit a pot hole or went around a corner, I'd sway into Michiko and squish her against the wall below the window. The bus jolted along. When it changed gears, I'd do this whiplash thing with my head. So it was a sway right, sway left, whiplash-whiplash dance between Michiko and me. I gave Michiko credit, though. She never once complained or looked embarrassed or said anything rude to me about it.

So there was the bus ride to survive, but also I'd never been so close to Michiko. I knew she played the violin and could read like a fish. In the past, arguing with her about the play didn't allow us much time for normal conversation. At one point on the thirty minute ride which always becomes much longer since the bus moved at the pace of icicles melting, Michiko pulled out a small sketch book and began drawing. I didn't know she was an artist.

"Oh, you draw. What is it?" I asked. What a stupid question. Anyone could tell she was drawing a tree—and a good one, too. Not like the ones I drew which looked like green lollipops with brown stick-looking trunks.

"It's a tree on a flat," Michiko remarked rather matter of fact, blocking my view with her shoulder.

"Oh, a piece of scenery?" I knew she knew I knew what a flat was. *Dumb, dumb...*I said to myself.

"Yes, a piece of scenery for our play. My father said when he met the other parents on the set committee they weren't confident about their drawing ability, so I volunteered to do it." She continued sketching, her dainty fingers stroking the paper in soft, squiggly lines.

I felt Bumbling Bea rising in my throat. Again.

Bumbling Bea wanted to say, "Don't you think you're going kinda' over the top on this play thing?" but I swallowed her back down and she retreated. This was good. I was beating my negative side, my threatened-by-Michiko side.

I took a chance since I thought that for once I was in charge of my brain. I relaxed and before I even knew it, Bumbling Bea erupted like Mt. Vesuvius but worse than ever. "Don't you think you're kinda' over the top on this play thing?" I snarled. Then Bumbling Bea, I mean, *I* added Peter's words (as if it wasn't bad enough all ready), "It's not like it's Broadway or something."

Ouch!

Michiko turned, looked at me sadly and whispered, "Why do you hate me so much, Beatrice?"

What was I to say? It wasn't Michiko that I didn't like. Truthfully, it was my alter ego that I didn't like. That was first and foremost. Michiko seemed to be a close second, however. I was clueless as to how to answer her.

How do you tell someone she irks you for no reason? She had more imagination and inventiveness in one of her teeny fingers than you did in your whole body on one of your best creative days? How could I compete with her amazing ideas and free spirit personality? I was none of those things. I was a scared, awkward, unsure girl worried about her future and missing her dad. Something about Michiko made me look at myself and I didn't like it.

I sat there with ecstatic students all around me. High school loomed ahead of me in the next ten months. I was uneasy to say the least. I had only two friends who, at the moment, were both furious with me. How would I survive the play, much less the rest of the year? Whether Michiko knew it or not, after the curtain closed on the play she was going to be super popular. I would be at home with no friends, eating left over flag dinners with my brother. She would be making gobs of "besties" and invited to everything on the popular kids' social calendars.

Even though Bumbling Bea appeared to be in charge of me, I knew I had to fix things with Michiko. I was about to confide to Michiko about my worries for my future nonexistent social life when our Yellow Dog came to a stuttering halt. Michiko jumped out of her seat, slipped by me and was first in line to exit the bus. I had blown my chance to apologize to her for what a drip I'd been and had made it worse by treating her badly on the ride.

We were given an hour and a half to look around the art museum, have lunch in the cafeteria (hamburgers and curly fries, of course) and walk over to the city theater close by--with our field trip partner walking right beside us.

Great.

"Beatrice, why don't you and Michiko lead our group over to the theater?" my helpful, unknowing mom suggested.

"Sure, Mom. Come on, Michiko it's this way," I chirped a little too brightly.

Michiko straightened her cat ears informing me, "The pedestrian crossing light turned green straight ahead of us. We should go that way," she pointed her teeny finger the other direction.

Here we go again. Another argument about nothing. A crosswalk light? You got to be kidding me! I'm the one from the United States and I should know which way is better to do...everything here, like the best way to walk to a theater. Bumbling Bea snarked aloud, "Certainly, Miss Michiko, whatever you say."

As we continued crossing the street according to Michiko's opinion, she suddenly stopped mid street and said quietly, "I give in. You lead the group, Miss Beatrice," she mocked me. "You know what's best all the time anyway."

I'd had it! "Listen, if you think I'm going to turn around a group of twenty-five eighth graders right in the middle of the street and walk the other way, you are completely nuts." I snarled.

Michiko stopped and glared at me. "I'm talking about the play. You are the stage manager. I should be quiet and listen to you and Ms. Phillips. It is unimportant what I think. I'm the new student at school. I know you think I'm weird and pushy and overly dramatic and, and..."

Now I know you won't believe this, but we were standing right in the middle of the street with all of the rest of the kids in our group circled around us. Honestly, we were. A few cars tooted their horns, but we all stood there stunned by Michiko's outburst. Michiko looked around at the crowd informing us, "I come from a family of theater people on my father's side. Theater is tremendously important to me. In fact, it's everything to me. I take it seriously and I care about every inch of it." She dropped her head and hefted her beloved pink backpack on her shoulder.

"Michiko, do you and Beatrice have a problem with each other?" my wonderful mother corralled the stragglers at the end of the group. "Let's continue on across the street and then solve it. A policeman is watching us."

The group melted away into pods of whispers and jeers so as not to cause any more commotion than we already had. Michiko walked ahead with Jerri and Peter. I stayed behind with my mother. I wished at least I'd joined some of the other kids that were walking along by themselves, but they didn't seem too keen on including me either. Double great.

The only person who would talk to me was Mom. She was about the last one I wanted to talk to, however. She put her arm around my shoulders. "I don't know what has come over you in the past few months, Beatrice, but I wish you'd get ahold of yourself and behave like the great girl I know. You've become such a meanie."

I didn't defend myself to her. I had no come back for that remark.

During the play, (*Romeo and Juliet*—did I tell you?) which should have been all exciting for me because it's my favorite of Shakespeare's, I sat on the back row of the balcony section near the sound booth and watched the technician manage cues and microphones. I wanted the field trip to be over so we could go back to school and go home.

At intermission my mother asked Ms. Phillips, "So, how is the play going? Beatrice told me that she was having a good time working on it."

WHAT? I SAID NO SUCH THING.

"Is that so?" Ms. Phillips gave me a subtle stare. I don't think Mom noticed. "Beatrice is invaluable help to all of us. I know that Michiko appreciates her stage managing. She has mentioned to me several times that she looks forward to having Beatrice help her rehearse tomorrow. You know, they are rehearsal partners."

"Yes, Beatrice told me. I think this has been a good lesson in patience and understanding. Don't you, Beatrice?" Mom nodded at me.

I angrily stared at my program, if you can do that to a program. Mostly, I wanted to scream. Boy, I hate it when parents do that. They put words in your mouth.

Although I have to say that if I had it all together, I would have said the patient and understanding thing myself except I didn't have it all together. I think my mom knew that.

Fortunately, the second act was super short (they cut out a bunch of stuff) and after curtain call (at which the popular kids hooted and hollered like they were at an all-star basketball game—*so* embarrassing), we filed out.

I had to catch up with Michiko who desperately needed the bathroom. Lucky me.

I never know what to do when I'm waiting for a friend using the bathroom, do you? Do you wait outside the bathroom or stand inside by the sinks and observe the cleaning procedures of other people washing their hands? You feel like the Hand Washing Police. You can't stand by the hand dryer or the exit door, because you're in the way. So, I did the next best thing, I thought. I stood right in front of Michiko's stall door, leaning against it. The bathroom was kinda small and I kept pushing against the stall door to get out of the way of other bathroom users.

It took Michiko forever in the stall. The stall door lock jiggled, then stopped.

"I'm locked in. I can't get out. Oh, no..." Michiko uttered weakly. She rattled the door a bunch of times, but nothing budged.

Michiko was right. She was stuck.

Great.

Chapter Ten

Yup, Michiko was stuck and it was sort of my fault.

Luckily, all the girls from the field trip cleared out of the bathroom, so we were alone. "Michiko, is something wrong? Earlier I was mean to you and I'm sorry. I say dumb things and do dumb things." I suggested, "We need to go. I mean, get out of here. The bus is waiting for us. If we're too late, the bus driver leaves without us."

Michiko's voice was steady and hushed. I barely heard her through the door. "I'm locked in, Beatrice. The door won't open," she explained. "And besides, it's not you. It's me. I loved the play. I always love each play I attend or read. I was jealous, too. I wanted to be the girl playing Juliet kneeling there looking out at the audience whispering, 'Yea, noise? Then I'll be brief. Oh happy dagger. This is thy sheath. There rust and let me die.'"

I was listening at the stall door when Michiko dramatically recited Juliet's last few words. If anyone walked in on us, I was sure this would be a strange sight. Bumbling Bea thought so, but I didn't care. It was the way Michiko recited Juliet's words. She was so convincing. At school I was distracted by Michiko's antics and I never listened very closely to her. With the door between us, I had no choice *but* to listen. You know what? At that moment, Juliet Capulet was standing on the opposite side of that door mourning for her love, and I wanted to help her. Michiko, I mean.

"It's okay. We are gonna' be fine. Someone will realize we're not on the bus and tell my mother..."

My dear sweet mother walked in on us. "Beatrice, where's Michiko? I told the bus driver go on ahead without us. I called Dad's secretary but he was teaching. So I called Mr. Tannabe and he was busy, so he called Mrs. Tannabe who will pick us up instead. She'll be here in a while. Her migraine is better. Are you two okay?"

This was humiliating for both Michiko and me, so I covered with, "We are better than okay, Mom. We're terrific, right Michiko?"

My mom gave me a look. It said, "There is more to this story than you are telling me, but I'll wait until we're home." Personally, I think those are the worst kind of looks.

"Mother is coming? Oh, no," Michiko sniffed.

I didn't understand Michiko's worry, but I was relieved. We were over the misunderstanding as quickly as the janitor came and loosened the door lock. I couldn't blame this one on my parents. This was *my* fault. Not even Bumbling Bea's.

In my effort to stay out of the way of the other restroom users, my leaning against Michiko's stall door had jammed it. Figures. You gotta give me some credit, though. For once I said the right thing and it felt good.

Ha! Take that, Meanie Bea. I thought.

Chapter Eleven

Even though Michiko and I settled our differences, she was quiet and stayed to herself at rehearsal the next day. I think it was because of her mother's conversation with my mom on the ride home from the theater field trip.

I met Michiko's mother at our house when her family came over that one time. She was dainty like Michiko, with jet black hair coiffed in a swirly bun of some kind. It was perfect. Not a stray hair out of place. She wore black like no one I'd ever seen—black top and sweater, slacks, and shoes. Even her earrings were black which was kind of a waste since her black hair competed with it and won.

"Did Michiko make a great fuss at the play?" Mrs. Tannabe asked. She quickly explained to mom about the whole family in theater thing. "I bet she told you about her family performing in theater for many years. My husband's brother is a famous Kabuki actor in Japan. In the past, one could only become a Kabuki actor if another male family member had been one before him. My husband's great grandfather, his grandfather and father were Anagato actors. Those are the men who portray the female characters. Like my brother in law, they were celebrated actors of their time."

My mom chimed in, "Yes, I know a little about it. Weren't women the first to create Kabuki? For hundreds of years after the men took over, they played both the male and female roles."

"My husband's brother continues the family tradition. Sho's brother is the older sibling of the two of them and began his Kabuki acting training as a young boy. We received an email from him. He has decided to retire from performing. It's taxing to the performer's body and, what with his arthritis, his body cannot endure it any longer."

"So that's why Michiko has such a bent for performing," my mom smiled excitedly. "It is so fascinating that both men chose a career in dramatic arts. How interesting that your husband became a professor of theater. Although I don't know your husband well, it seems to suit him."

"I'm not certain that he thinks so, though," Mrs. Tannabe looked at the rear view mirror leering at Michiko and saying sternly, "Michiko knows there is no future in it for her since she's female, but she persists on studying it anyway. Why should she go through all the years of studying Kabuki and not be able to perform in it? Better to be more practical and make a good living that doesn't destroy your health." Mrs. Tannabe quickly changed the subject and discussed our upcoming disaster—I mean our play.

Michiko was so distant and introverted. She didn't talk to me or our mothers the whole ride home, but stared out of the car window muttering to herself.

I kept quiet because I'd gotten myself into enough trouble for one day. Luckily, Bumbling Bea was asleep in her dragon lair for the time being.

Michiko shifted in her seat and took out a worn copy of *Romeo and Juliet*. If she could have made herself any smaller than she already was, she'd have been a dot. She curled up her teeny slender legs and gently set the book on her lap as if it was a fragile flower.

Michiko must have sensed my curiosity. Plopping her cat ears very defiantly on her head while fiercely keeping her eyes on her mother she whispered, "I'll explain more tomorrow, Beatrice."

So, I waited.

Chapter Twelve

Guess what? The most amazing thing happened to me the next day. Remember Bronson, the new boy at school? He sat by me in Science class—ALL ON HIS OWN! No matter what happened at school that day, I would survive it because Beautiful Bronson noticed me. Wow!

Rehearsal began as it always did. I took roll. Three cast members were absent, supposedly with the flu. Ms. Phillips told us all to take care of ourselves and eat our fruits and vegetables. I thought that was a funny comment coming from Ms. Phillips because I'd never seen her with any real food in her hand but a diet cola or a few potato chips.

Since the play was right around the corner, Ms. Phillips breezed through the beginning parts and told the cast they should read it over on their own and make decisions as to what they wanted to do. She said something about "organic acting"-- whatever that was. This was a strange direction coming from Ms. Phillips because I'd never had a director give a cast the permission to do what they wanted to in a production. We were desperate to get through it. I only hoped nothing strange happened.

We skipped to the end of the play to John Smith's proposal to Pocahontas. Well, we tried to. As usual, Michiko stopped the rehearsal and she demanded a rewrite of the play.

"As I mentioned before, Ms. Phillips the story is inaccurate. A lot of things happened to Pocahontas. She was captured by the English settlers, married another man named John Rolfe and so forth. She never married John Smith. The historians aren't convinced that she defended him at all, but maybe Powhatan set it all up."

There was a huge sigh from the cast, but not from me.

Principal Wells stepped in. "Michiko is right, Ms. Phillips. I've been meaning to speak to you about this. I promised you I'd stay in the background. However, my character, Powhatan could be the one to blame for the bogus information. More focus should be put upon my character. "

Someone snickered, imitating Principal Wells with a "Bogus?"

Does anyone say 'bogus' anymore?

I began to see both sides of the situation. Do we go ahead and present the play as it was written or fix it?

"I agree with Michiko, Ms. Phillips." I stepped beside Michiko teaming up with her. Bumbling Bea didn't like that too much and I felt that odd feeling in my stomach that came with a BB eruption, but I held fast to my real self and took a big breath.

"I trusted my college friend to make the edits we needed. He did a nice job on the play. At this point, we must go ahead with the production as planned," Ms. Phillips reflected worriedly, "Perhaps we could inform the audience that we're presenting a fable about Pocahontas rather than…"

Suddenly, Michiko yelled, "No, no. We must tell the story the right way. The authentic way! There could be audience members who don't know the story. If we don't tell it correctly, I can't…." Michiko dropped her script and stuttered, "---and my uncle will be…" and quickly left the stage, heading out of the auditorium doors.

Something was terribly wrong. I didn't need Ms. Phillips to tell me to follow Michiko. I slipped into the hallway in time to see Michiko's petite hand push the girls' bathroom door closed.

WHAT'S THE DEAL WITH US AND BATHROOMS?

I pushed the door open to find Michiko sitting under the hand dryers on her beloved pink backpack. She looked at me through a veil of hair that fell over her face. Her bird-like legs were crossed in front of her.

"I know what you think, Beatrice. You think I'm ridiculous, right? Go on, say it."

Bumbling Bea was nowhere to be found. Unbelievable. I thought, *Maybe if I distract Michiko, I can get her out of here.*

"Michiko, I don't think you are ridiculous. Wearing cat ears all the time is crazy, but you aren't ridiculous." Looking for something to laugh about I joked, "At least I won't lock you in the stall like last time. It's safer for us to talk out here, huh?"

She sighed a little, relaxing her shoulders. "It's that...my mother told my father I created a scene on the field trip. She threatened to pull me out of the play as punishment for embarrassing the family. My mother hates me." Michiko's dark eyes watered. She was on the verge of crying. "My mother doesn't understand me. She never has understood me. I wear cat ears just to annoy her and because I like them. She thinks I'm trying to get my way, because I want to be in Kabuki Theater when I grow up. She requires me to play violin because she played it. She thinks it makes a person more cultured. Why doesn't acting make a person more cultured? If anyone should understand culture, it's an actor." Michiko raised her fists and punched her backpack behind her. "She wants me to be a scientist or a doctor. I find those subjects tiresome and monotonous." She continued, "I have no interest in those careers at all. I want to be a storyteller like my uncle and grandfathers before him and tell stories on a stage. There is nothing better than dramatizing one's thoughts through a play, don't you agree?"

I didn't know what to say to that. I felt like I walked into an argument she was having with her mother right then and there. She was way ahead of me in understanding her passion for the stage. I looked at the play as a way to edge closer to the popular kids and get attention from my father, but she saw it as a personal gift she shared with an audience.

Have you ever said something that was important and sounded like a grown up, but you didn't even think it? It sort of came out? I became, *Magnificent* Bea! Magnificent Bea showed up for the first time. I was clueless where Bumbling Bea was hiding and I didn't care.

Magnificent Bea said, "Look, the play is next week. You're doing a good job. The production is unusual this year and it's because you are a part of it. You make us all think about it instead of participating so we can go on the New York trip. The show is only a few days away. Can you keep away from your mom and sort of stay under her radar until then?"

I, Magnificent Bea, thought of something else, "Hey, I have a stick of bright red lipstick. I bought it for its name—Razz Ma Jazz Red. I've never even used it. I saw this in a movie once. You wanna' kiss the mirror with it?"

Michiko tilted her head. "Because why?"

"Because it's a little bad," I warned. "You seem like a rule follower and so am I most of the time," I admitted. "Have you ever done anything wild? Kissing the mirror in Razz Ma Jazz Red isn't breaking the law, but it's a little crazy and if we do it quickly and get outta' here, no one will know who did it. It'll be our little secret. What ya' think, Miss Michiko?" I challenged her.

Michiko stood, pushed her hair out of her face, pulled on her jacket, and buttoned it. Putting her delicate hand out for the lipstick she declared, "I'd like to go first, Miss Beatrice, if you don't mind."

I bowed dramatically, extending my hand with the lipstick.

We guessed how to do the meaningless crime. I'm not sure it was right, but we felt awfully wicked. After ringing our lips with the waxy red stuff, we took turns kissing the mirror up, down, left and right.

"Oh John Smith, I love you sooo much!" Michiko squeaked laughingly.

"You love Peter?" I teased her.

"No. Peter? Hardly. " Her eyes got all dreamy. "I love the idea of John Smith. He took a smart girl and showed her the world. How romantic." Michiko crooned.

We both giggled at Peter's expense. We were busy kissing the mirror and didn't hear the bathroom exit door open or see Ms. Phillips standing there watching us.

"Girls, what are you two doing?" Ms. Phillips cocked her head at us, miffed. "Clean this up and you two go home. Rehearsals finished early for the day. Again." She mumbled as she left the bathroom.

You know how you shouldn't laugh when you're in trouble because it makes the situation worse? Well, we flunked that one.

Chapter Thirteen

It was Monday and in two days we perform the play. Last weekend, Bronson came over to my house and we played a board game with Edmund. Yes, you read that right. BRONSON CAME OVER TO MY HOUSE!! I called Michiko to see if she would like to join us, but her mother said that she was ill. It was probably the flu, I guessed.

On Monday morning, I looked for Michiko but Jerri told me (we were speaking again, thankfully) that Michiko wasn't in their first hour P.E. class. Maybe she was only late to school?

At lunch, I asked Peter (we were also speaking again, thankfully) if he'd seen her but he hadn't.

At rehearsal I substituted for her in the play. I won't go into the details of all of it, but I was dreadful. The cast was nice enough not to say anything about my puny performance. After watching Michiko portray the role, I looked like a cardboard cutout.

"Beatrice, have you heard from Michiko? I hope she's back to-morrow or she can't be in the show— those pesky extra-curricular policies," Ms. Phillips nervously reminded me.

"She'll be here, Ms. Phillips. Michiko is fierce and determined." I didn't know if Michiko would be well enough to be in the play, but what do you say to a nervous director?

I rode over to Michiko's house right after rehearsal. I had to go. I still had her email letter and photo. I needed to give them to her and admit my keeping them from her.

"Please sit down, Beatrice," Mrs. Tannabe offered a chair to me. "Michiko is sleeping off the flu and I don't want to wake her. I'm sure you understand. You rode your bicycle all the way over here? The least we can do is get to know each other better. How about some cookies? Do you like hot tea?"

I wasn't much of a tea drinker, much less hot tea. I didn't know what to say so I did what I thought grownups would do. I smiled and nodded, noticing the extremely tidy and perfect room. Everything had a place and everything was in its proper place. My bedroom was a dusty mess ("organized chaos" my mother said) like, all the time. This room was spotless and perfect, like Mrs. Tannabe.

Perched on the shelf above the fireplace was a black and white photo of a Kabuki actor. Mrs. Tannabe was still in the kitchen, so I peered more closely at the face in the photo. Déjà vu. The face looked like the one in Michiko's email.

"That's Michiko's grandfather in the photo. He died when she was a baby. She never knew him. She thinks she knows him because she has heard so many stories about him from her father." Mrs. Tannabe brushed a piece of miniscule lint from her slacks.

We made small talk, which I'm terrible at, talking for several minutes about school and our families. I explained about my mother's career as an artist before she married my dad. She shared about her husband's teaching experiences and how Michiko had lived in several cities in the U.S.

Sometimes I don't know what to say, but I know what NOT to say and that comes out instead. For once lately, I didn't do that. I wasn't Bumbling Bea this time.

"So, Michiko tells me you aren't all that excited about her being in the school play. She is so good. Will you come see the show?"

Mrs. Tannabe pursed her lips and picked at an invisible knot on her perfect top. "This is her father's project. I hoped she would join the science club and would enjoy those pursuits instead. Theater is a waste of her time. Soon you girls will be going into high school and your grades will count for college. Michiko needs to begin preparing for her college admissions now. It's too late if you wait until you are further along in high school."

Huh? How did we get there? I was talking about the play and somehow Mrs. Tannabe took us to college! Nibbling on the yummy almond flavored cookies Mrs. Tannabe offered, I tried to put us back on the subject of the play.

"Uhm, I enjoy the Kabuki theater additions Michiko taught us."

"I didn't know Michiko had taken things that far. With Kabuki, I mean." Mrs. Tannabe declared. "Why can't that girl mind me?" she mumbled.

When she saw me staring at her, she gave a little laugh. "You must excuse me, Beatrice. I haven't spoken to a single soul all day and I guess I needed to talk. Would you like another cookie?"

Oh man, I was in too deep. Whenever that happens, Bumbling Bea takes over.

"I don't understand," Bumbling Bea said. "You mean Michiko isn't supposed to talk about Japan at all?"

Mr. Tannabe walked through the front door. His warm expression changed to a serious one when he saw me sitting there. "Hello, Beatrice. I'm guessing you came to see Michiko? The play is coming up, yes? So, what time is the curtain on Wednesday?"

I was sure Mr. Tannabe knew the time of the curtain. He seemed like someone who remembers and knows the 4-1-1 on everything.

Mr. Tannabe walked me out to the street where my bike lay. Suddenly, I remembered the email letter in my back pack. "Here, Mr. Tannabe. This belongs to Michiko. I wanted to give it to her myself. She was asleep and your wife..." I hesitated. "So I forgot. Could you give it to her?"

Mr. Tannabe took the letter from me whispering, "Please keep the letter and give it to her yourself. That would be best. Beatrice, you have been a good friend to Michie. I hope your time with us hasn't been too upsetting, but it will all work out. You'll understand soon." He handed the letter back to me.

Bumbling Bea wanted to say to him, "It's more confusing than upsetting. In fact, it's kinda' bewildering, you know?"

Instead I smiled and pedaled down the road waving backwards to Michiko's father. He laughed and when I glanced to see him, he was standing with his back turned to me waving backwards. Suddenly, I knew where Michiko got her sense of humor.

That had to do for the moment.

Chapter Fourteen

My Dad told me this weird thing called an "actor's nightmare." Sometimes an actor has a dream they are in a play but have on a costume from a whole different play. Or in the dream the actor can't remember his lines and when he happens to remember them, he speaks some foreign language that he doesn't even know or understand in real life. We all felt that way the day of the school play but not exactly in that order. At one point in our play, I wasn't absolutely positive that I wasn't asleep.

I left Michiko curled up in her Pocahontas costume looking more like a death shroud than a gown and jogged back and forth backstage dropping off props. "Remember, fifth graders, don't touch the props! And you better not eat them either—the corn husks aren't filled with candy corn or something, so stay away from them." I warned.

Jerri trudged behind me lugging a box of paper bag vests and feather head bands. We were close friends again and that made me super happy. "Yeah, and remember—if you can see the audience..."

"They can see you!" the smallest fifth grader chimed.

We finished making props and costume pieces and then tackled the Michiko problem. Propping Michiko on the piano bench I draped her costume over her shoulders and tapped her over heated cheek with a left over feather, "Michiko, it's time. Wake up."

At the hearing of her name, Michiko sat up quickly and emitted a loud sigh. "Yes, the show must go on. I am ready."

Jerri and I high fived each other hoping the plan we created last night would work.

Ms. Phillips was leering at us on the other side of the stage. "Beatrice, say places please," she instructed.

"And 'Break a Leg!'" Principal Wells loudly whispered.

Michiko blinked her eyes a couple of times and gave us a suspicious look, "Break whose leg?" She zeroed in on me. "Who are you? You sound like my friend, Beatrice but you are dressed very weirdly. She wears tee shirts with cartoon characters on them and high top basketball shoes."

Taking Michiko's over heated teeny face in my hands, I whispered, "I'm dressed as one of John Smith's men. I'm going to stand beside you like I'm your escort."

Michiko snorted a little laugh.

Peter jogged by looking oh, so John Smith-ly with his gallant entourage of seventh and eighth graders straggling behind him. "Break a leg, ladies," he exalted giving us a swift bow as he slid into his place on the stage. "I hope your plan works, Beatrice, because if not, I don't know what we'll do."

I ignored him and whispered to Michiko, "Jerri is going to be hiding behind you with her script in case you forget your lines. And Bronson is right in the wings if you need extra help. He's there to distract the fifth graders." We'd drafted Bronson to help us keep the fifth graders quiet backstage with paper air planes he fashioned out of extra play programs.

"No need for that, kind sir," Michiko assured me. "I am an actress. I can do this without your help, person-that–sounds-like-my-friend-Beatrice-but-looks-a-little-more-like-William-Shakespeare-with-a-bad-beard-and-mustache," she smirked. She stood bolt upright weaving a little in her thrift store moccasins. She shouted, "I, Michiko Tannabe, was born to play Pocahontas!"

The cast stared at her.

Noticing the stares, Michiko plopped on the piano bench. "What am I to do again if I forget my lines?"

Jerri instructed Michiko. "If you forget your lines, I won't help you out right away. Remember to say something similar to the line you've spaced out on. You know, wing it."

Squeaky pulleys that hoisted the ropes opened the big dusty red velvet curtain and somebody sneezed.

We were on.

Surprisingly, the first ten minutes of the play went pretty well. The fifth grade boys did as they were coached, leaving each other alone and didn't add a death scene early on in the play as they wanted.

I forgot what I was doing, I was enjoying my role so much. "Hear, Hear!" I improvised at one point. I twirled the ends of my fake brown mustache and scratched at my chin through my curly red beard (thanks to Dad's costume department's help).

We neared the last quarter of the play and it seemed like we would make it to curtain call without any problems.

"Remember, we help Michiko stand near the end of the play," I reminded Jerri earlier. "We'll take about two steps downstage away from the piano bench. You keep your hands clamped around Michiko's waist, steadying her from behind."

Michiko looked more like a state fair princess riding on a parade float than Pocahontas, but hey, we were working it!

For the first time all evening, she looked at the audience, smiling weakly at the audience in the fourth row. "Oh, no," Michiko mumbled.

I looked out at the audience and saw who Michiko was staring at--beside her father there was another man who looked a lot like Mr. Tannabe, except older. He sat in rapt attention to her.

Michiko pulled away from us and took a slow graceful cross to Peter. "I can do this after all. I don't need your help. I feel fine, Beatrice," Michiko whispered.

She was going to make it. We were in the homestretch—go Michiko!

To be safe, Jerri and I followed her close behind. Michiko stopped. Tipping her head ever so slightly, like I saw her practice in rehearsal she opened her mouth as if to speak. I said "as if to speak" because at first, nothing came out.

Nothing. Nada.

No words came out of Michiko's mouth. More of an "Uh, um, err..."

"What do we do?" Jerri whispered to me but before I could answer, Jerri ducked under the back stage curtain.

What a sight. There stood Michiko in her oversized Pocahontas costume. I was wrong-she looked more like a ghost than a state fair princess. Raising her regal head, she surveyed the audience, buying time for her memory to kick in, I imagined. Instead of Pocahontas' lines, she recited Shakespeare's:

"Love is not love

Which alters when it alteration finds,

Or bends with the remover to remove.

O, no! It is an ever-fixed mark,

That looks on tempests and is never shaken.

It is the star to every wandering bark,

whose worth's unknown, although his height be taken."

WHAT THE HECK?

The moment froze in time. It was exactly like the first rehearsal day when we thought Michiko had a seizure or something.

Michiko lifted her right arm above her head and turned in her father's direction. Opening her eyes wide and crossing them, she jiggled her head a bit and struck that mie pose I'd read about on the internet.

I was wrong. Two people *did* move--Principal Wells and me. When Michiko stepped away from us, Jerri and I were stuck on stage. Jerri did the usual Jerri thing and ducked behind the stage left curtain. I tried to hide myself by sliding on my stomach under the upstage curtain.

Oops. Bumbling Bea strikes again.

I forgot about Principal Wells who was also backstage in case we needed him. Running into him, I thought quick enough to utter, "Oh, excuse me."

Principal Wells replied with a gentlemanly, "Most probab-" bowing to me as he backed against the stage wall. Principal Wells was a tall brawny man--there wasn't much room for his muscled shoulders or his boat sized feet and he tripped on a gymnastic mat. Or rather, he tripped on one of the left over gymnastic mats I couldn't get rammed in the closet!

I thought I heard a loud ripping sound like a cardboard box splitting at its seams.

Yes, it *was* a cardboard box splitting at its seams!

How could it be so rock-band loud?

The red kick balls I placed in the box on top of the shelf above the wayward gymnastic mat bounced out, escaping onto the stage. Springing red gum ball looking things scattered around the stage like giant billiard balls hit with a cue stick. One even bounced off the stage and into the aisle of paparazzi parents.

Vroom! A squadron of program paper airplanes from stage right sailed over us like miniature glider planes that stalled and plummeted to the stage floor.

Bronson wrestled with one of the fifth grade boys in a strangle hold with one arm and a wayward paper airplane in the other. The little turd (not Bronson, the fifth grader) apologetically smiled at me, but his face looked more thrilled than sorry.

Without missing a beat, Michiko came out of the Kabuki trance saying to Peter, "I mean, yes. Sure. I'll marry you, John Smith."

Peter was so surprised by the paper airplanes, bouncing red kick balls and Michiko's strange freeze thing, he turned to me and let out a belly laugh-one I hadn't heard from him in a long time.

The curtain closed, the stage lights went out and there was huge applause and laughter from all of us. At curtain call, the cast included the red kick balls in their bows and dragged Jerri and I on the stage, placing us right beside Michiko and Peter.

I whispered out the side of my mouth at Michiko, "What the heck was that you said?"

Taking her bow, Michiko looked at me with a twinkle in her eye which made me think that maybe she planned it. She purposely messed up? She never admitted it to me. In her typical matter of fact way she replied, "I guess I am more ill than I thought. I couldn't remember the lines, but I could remember my favorite Shakespearean sonnet, number sixteen. I winged it. What did ya' think?"

It wasn't Dad's "actor's nightmare" after all.

Chapter Fifteen

I wish I could say the rest of the evening went well, but it didn't. About the time we were through cleaning the stage, my parents showed up. My wonderful mom was at the show all along, but it was obvious my dad breezed in at curtain call. I checked out the audience prior to the show and he was nowhere to be found.

"Great show, Beatrice," my tardy father said.

"I don't know how you can call it 'great' when you weren't even here to see it," I mumbled loud enough so he could hear it.

"You two have to work this out." Mom looked in my direction then waved to one of her arts friends leaving the two of us alone.

The moment had arrived and I was ready. I didn't realize I was prepared until I blurted, "See what you have done? Mom left us alone here. She is tired of your disinterest in us and she is making me tell you what I think of you."

"Beatrice, I had a dress rehearsal for my production at the university. I am a director, remember? I can't walk out and leave the show to run itself." My father rubbed his forehead and sank tiredly on one of the chairs.

"Oh, that's rich, Dad. You can walk out on us and leave us to take care of ourselves, but you can't walk out on some precious play telling a pretend story? Edmund and I are the real thing, Dad, in case you have forgotten. You have a stage manager. You are always telling me how you can't survive without a stage manager. How about she takes over for an evening and you put us first for once?"

Now you might think my anger was ridiculous because I, myself, spent the last two weeks putting together a play like my dad. BUT, mine was different, obviously.

"Bea, it isn't that easy and you know it," he reminded me.

I huffed, "Well, it is to me. To us. If you would only come home and be with us, everything would be all...." I stopped in mid-sentence. Was this me speaking or Bumbling Bea?

Dad gave me one of his sheepish grins which usually worked on me to see things his way, but not this time. "Beatrice, I love you and Edmund. Nothing will change that. I still have things in my life to sort out. Mom and I agreed to give this separation a year. The year ends on January first. I have responsibilities other than the family. I have other passions, too. Mom and I owe it to ourselves to see this through and wait until January to make any decisions. You know this. Nothing I am saying to you should be a surprise to you." He stood trying to hug me, but I stepped away. "I know I missed the show. I know I hurt your feelings by not seeing the show and I know that you and Edmund are confused by me. Please give me time." He quickly walked away and left me alone. Again.

I wish I could turn my ears off when people say certain things to me I don't want to hear.

The popular kids appeared at about at the time my dad was finished whining at me but I am sure they heard all the juicy nitty gritty stuff. So did Bumbling Bea.

"Hysterical show, Beatrice," one said.

"The bouncing balls were hilarious. Did you think of that?" another added.

I don't know where Bumbling Bea came from, but she was back. I cocked my head like one of those dolls whose head jiggles and smirked, "Oh, you guys liked that touch? Yeah, I thought of it." I couldn't get stopped. I bragged, "It was something I wanted to try this year because the show is always so boring. I asked Ms. Phillips if it would be all right with her and she thought it was a fabulous idea."

Okay, so I exaggerated a bit.

Michiko appeared from backstage carrying left over paper airplanes. She looked at me quizzically. "What are you saying, Beatrice? You didn't think up that stuff. I did. I did what I had to do when Peter forgot his lines. The rest of it was by accident."

Lying? I'd never heard Michiko lie before.

I flipped my hair over my shoulder like I'd seen Miss Popular do a dozen times before. "Hey, we're all going to my house for a little after show party. You wanna' come too?"

"Sure," the girl agreed, but seemed disinterested.

I wouldn't say that I was being opportunistic—that's a person who jumps on a remarkable chance to be successful. But for once in my life, I had paid attention to the circumstances and worked things out to my advantage. Wow, I was so rockin' it!

"Cool. I'm done here anyway. Let's go. See ya' later, Michiko," I grabbed my things hurrying out the door.

Oh my gosh, popular kids were coming over to my house for a party! I thought. There was no way I was gonna' miss a chance to be with them.

I thought Michiko didn't hear me, because she followed me out to the car Mom was driving me home in, for once.

Michiko slipped her arm through Starr's arm, the leader popular girls. "I'm so glad you are coming to the party, too. Beatrice invited me earlier."

I DID?

Chapter Sixteen

It's true. I had invited Michiko to my party. I forgot about it. And I invited Bronson, Peter and Jerri, too. I was so excited that Starr (honestly, that's her name) and her buddies were coming.

"Okay, kids pile in!" my mom cheered.

Michiko, still glued to Starr, pushed past me to the middle of our car sitting between Starr and her other BFFs. I say "other BFFs" because it was clear to me even though I was the one having the party, I was forgotten.

"Want some cheese curls, you guys?" Opening her backpack, Michiko pulled out an enormous bag of the nearly neon puffed curly snack. "My mother will never buy them for me. She thinks the orange coloring is toxic. So, I bought them myself. I only get veggie chips at my house."

"Could I have some, Michiko?" I tried to smile like the other girls.

Michiko threw her blue black hair over her shoulder as I had, and exactly like Starr. "Oh, sorry Beatrice. I thought you weren't allowing yourself to have these since you are on that diet."

WHAT?

"Good for you, Beatrice. Don't wanna' get pudgy right as we go into high school next year," reminded one of the other popular girls who was wearing *cat ears*.

Michiko spilled my beans and I was stunned. One day after school, I admitted to her about planning to go on a diet.

"It's a secret, Michiko. Please don't tell anyone," I pleaded. "I hate how I look and I'm trying to curb my obsession with malted milk balls."

"You look good the way you are, Beatrice. You don't need to diet." Her compliment seemed so sincere at the time.

That was then. Today was a whole different day.

One of the girls gushed, "Michiko, you're an amazing actress. Someday, you are definitely going to be a star. I've never seen anything like it, have you guys?" One of the girls said to the others.

Michiko sneezed and attacked me. "Yuck, who has on disgusting perfume? Is it you, Beatrice? I told you I'm allergic to it. It's your entire fault I sneezed, you idiot." She turned to the others and they all laughed.

Idiot? When did I become an idiot?

Something bizarre was going on with Michiko. She sounded like Bumbling Bea-- not herself. Why was she copying me?

Peter, Bronson, and Jerri were sitting on the porch by my front door when we arrived home. "Hey, let's go downstairs and watch some funny video clips. There's an awesome one where a cheerleader falls off a human pyramid and her butt shows." Peter suggested.

"It's a riot!" Michiko wailed.

I didn't know Peter watched videos on line. I didn't know Michiko did either. And I didn't know Michiko already knew Starr and her buddies. Even though it was my house and all, I followed the rest of the group to the basement where Jerri was setting up some drinks and snacks.

We watched the video clips for a while. Most of them were mean or stupid—one was of a baby pig that had gotten its head stuck in a fence and the momma pig squealed for what seemed like an hour until the farmer rescued it. My friends thought the clips were hysterical, taking turns like dominoes toppling, doubling over in laughter. Michiko laughed the loudest. I stared at my friends.

"Hey, let's dance!" cheered Peter.

Peter dances?

Michiko ran over to Peter and began dancing with him. Suddenly they took hands and did a tango kind of thing. Some other girl grabbed Bronson and did the same.

My friends never act like this. Maybe it's having the popular kids at the party? I thought.

About the time Michiko exhausted Peter with all her tango-ing, she pushed me out of the way, cut in between the girl and Bronson and grabbed his hand. Twirling herself toward him, she yelled over the music, "Sorry, Beatrice. I hope you won't get jealous and all. I know how much you like Bronson!"

They all stared at me, except for Bronson. For a big guy, Bronson did an impressive job of shrinking to the size of a peanut. He was so embarrassed. I was so embarrassed. Michiko kept singing to the music, "Oh baby, you make my heart all a flutter like no other..."

I was furious. I stepped in the way of the dancers, demanding, "Michiko, I need to talk to you. NOW." I stressed.

Bronson slunk away from Michiko and busied himself with the potato chip bowl. Peter whispered to Bronson, "Oh my gosh, buddy. Did you know Beatrice felt that way?" Bronson shrugged his shoulders and ate chips one by one.

Although the music was blaring, the room was silent around it. Only Michiko continued dancing. She looked as ridiculous as I felt.

I tried again, "Michiko, I need to talk to you. RIGHT NOW." I grabbed her spaghetti thin arm and dragged her to the only private place in the basement—the bathroom. Calling it a bathroom is an overstatement. It's more like a closet with a turquoise sink and a pink toilet my dad switched out from the upstairs bathroom when he attempted to remodel the basement.

"You guys..." I tried to figure out what to say next to my party guests. Looking at Jerri, I suggested, "There are old board games in the closet. You know where they are, Jerri. Help yourself. I need to talk to Michiko for a minute," I slammed the door.

I forgot that the bathroom light bulb had blown a couple of days ago. Standing in the dark with only the glow of a night light, I was nose to nose with Michiko. Yes, in a bathroom again.

"What are you doing, Michiko?"

"What do you mean?" Michiko checked her outfit turning one way and then the other.

"Let me put it this way. You sound more like Bumbling Bea…I mean you sound more like me than you."

"I'm having fun. Beatrice, you aren't the only person who can do that." Michiko fluffed her hair a bit, straightening her cat ears.

"But you told the others some stuff that you promised not to tell anyone. I asked you to keep it a secret."

"I forgot," she sneezed again.

"You and the popular kids seem like best friends. I didn't even know you knew them. And I don't wear smelly perfume either."

"Well, maybe you should! Fix yourself up a little, Beatrice. High school is right around the corner and you're going to need to look and be sharp if you want to have a bunch of friends. Your black tee shirts and basketball shoes aren't exactly high fashion." She sneezed.

Her last comment stung me. I thought I looked cool and authentic—like I expressed myself through my clothing. She even dressed like me one day when her mom was out of town.

The doorbell rang, but we ignored it.

The bathroom door opened quickly and Michiko's mother interrupted us. "Michiko, what are you doing? You were to call me when the play was over and be home an hour ago."

Michiko swung around and faced her mother. "What does it look like I'm doing, Mother? Beatrice invited me to her party so I came along." She snuck a look at the other kids who had collected their things and begun to leave. Nothing like an argument to spoil the fun.

As we came upstairs, I heard Mom talking to Mrs. Tannabe about the play. "It was so wonderful, Mrs. Tannabe. I'm sorry that you missed it."

"Thank you for your concern, but I'm not at all sorry." She grabbed Michiko's violin case and spoke something under her breath in Japanese. Michiko blushed immediately. She turned to us. "Michiko, say thank you and let us go," she grumbled.

Michiko muttered "Thanks," leaving us quietly.

When Michiko stepped into the car, she slammed her door. Her mother glared at her as sped off down our driveway.

We watched them. "That door slam didn't sound very happy. Michiko seems different. Beatrice, what happened at the party?"

"Nothing, Mom. Michiko was acting weird. She said all kinds of things that didn't even sound like her." The more I talked, the angrier I became. "She was exaggerating and bragging a bunch. She told the entire world how I felt about Bronson. I tried to talk to her about it, but she wouldn't listen. Here I was trying to help her and she told me to mind my own business."

"Sounds like you, lately," Mom suggested grabbing an empty garbage can as she trudged up the back porch steps.

I defended myself. "What do you mean? I don't sound like that. It was so humiliating, Mother. When Michiko would say something weird, she'd give me a look to see if I was listening."

"Haven't you heard, 'Imitation is the highest form of flattery'?" Mom turned off the front porch light and locked the door. "Maybe she wants to be like you because she likes you."

*Who would ever want to be like Bumbling Bea? That's not me. Bumbling Bea is sarcastic and a know it all and exaggerates to make herself look good and...*I thought.

Oh, no.

Chapter Seventeen

"Hey, Michiko! Come sit here by me." Starr insisted the next day patting an imaginary spot on the lunch room benches.

If Michiko wasn't with one of her new popular friends someone other new popular friend took her place. "Wait for me, Michiko," she called from her locker sliding into place by her, too.

Mostly, I was sad. Michiko was my friend first until everyone else discovered her. I felt dumped. I thought about Shakespeare's quote, "All the world's a stage and all the people in it merely players." Maybe Shakespeare was right. Maybe Michiko was putting on an act in order to survive her life? It was clear to us that some of the Tannabe family didn't get along with each other. Nothing was worse than seeing a family argue right in front of you, especially when you hoped it would never come to that. Unfortunately, we saw the conflict more than once. They argued everywhere. They wore it like a rain coat on a rainy day-protecting themselves with it.

I was lucky. My parents didn't argue, at least not around us. But the difference was Michiko's parents were still living in the same house while mine were living apart. I don't know which was better. Time would tell. I decided that I would try to give back Michiko's note and photo and attempt to talk with Michiko during the party. That would be about the only time other people get some attention, like Peter for instance. Everyone who has ever played the lead character, even after the show is over, knows it's an important position that only fades with time and the next show's cast list. All eyes were on you.

After school was the cast party. Usually, I love cast parties. I think they are better than birthday parties. Cast parties feel like it's the entire cast's birthday all at once. The presents that you pretty much give yourself are unusual and most "normal" people wouldn't appreciate them or why you'd hold onto them with such care: your beloved, battered script that has fifty scribbled autographs from the cast and crew, or a card board sword you got to carry on stage in one scene for about fifteen seconds or a brand new pair of vintage shoes you found at a thrift store. You know, that sort of thing.

The cast party food was awesome, too. Big boxes of cheap pizza, gobs of different cookies, all the brownies and cakes that you could hope for plus crazy flavored cans of soda inviting you to guzzle them. I suppose a cast party for kids is something like a grown up's version of New Year's Eve.

"Hooray for us," we'd say, congratulating each other with wild abandon.

Ms. Phillips' classroom was tiny but we didn't care. Someone turned on a CD player and the show's music played. The song's lyrics weren't too catchy-- "Blessed Be the Tie That Binds" and we loudly sang along. It wasn't much but hey, we felt mighty proud.

Ms. Phillips stood on her desk chair. Her voice quavered a little bit. I thought she was going to cry. "Cast and crew, I am so proud of you. I know that the play production has always been a requirement in order to travel on the New York school trip, but you made me proud tonight. I'm excited to share with you that Principal Wells and I decided from now on we are going to present a different play each year."

Lots of us cheered and someone asked, "No more Pocahontas and John Smith?"

Mrs. Phillips laughed, "No more Pocahontas and John Smith. Maybe we'll produce *Alice in Wonderland* or *Tom Sawyer*. But whatever we do, it will never compare to our show. It was unusual to say the least."

From the back of the room Peter shouted, "Next year, can you work the red kick balls into it?"

We laughed. I looked for Michiko to see if she was laughing, too. I hoped she relaxed and was back to herself again.

I looked around at the party and didn't see her. There was only one place she'd be—the stage. So, I slipped out of the classroom and headed for the auditorium. What an eerie scene: I found Michiko on the stage standing all alone with only one light that shone on her from above. She hummed some odd tune and moved more like a dancer than an actor.

A man's voice called out, "Michie, more facial expression! Bring your knees higher. This is the most important part of the story. Have you been practicing? It looks to me like you haven't."

"Yes, Uncle. There hasn't been much time lately to practice. I'm sorry. I apologize." Seeing me, she choked out, "Beatrice, I didn't see you there."

"Hi, Michiko. Are you coming to the cast party? The whole cast is there and there's lots of food and ..." I stopped. It dawned on me why the man looked so familiar. He was the Kabuki actor in the photo that I kept and hadn't returned. Oh...

Her uncle interrupted me, "Michiko needs to practice and we can't rehearse at her home. Would you like to join us? We'll teach you what she is doing."

"Sure. But I have something to give to Michiko before we do." I dug in my back pocket and pulled out the battered envelope with the letter and photo.

Looking at my hand, she gave me a little smile, "Oh that. I knew you had them. Who else would?"

"I'm sorry, Michiko. I didn't like you at the time and well..."

Michiko gently took my hand. "It didn't matter to me that you had them. I have lots of letters from Uncle and photos, too. Besides if my mother found out that my uncle was still writing to me, she would have been furious. She is a snoop. She likes to go through my things when I am not home. So my uncle sends letters to me at my father's office address instead."

Wow. Michiko's father was in on Michiko's scheme, too.

Michiko's eyes beamed with excitement. "I would love to show you Kabuki. Would you like to learn?"

I tried my best to copy Michiko's Kabuki acting, but it was hard to do and complicated. I'd attempt to stand on one foot like her, but lost my balance pretty quickly. Her uncle demonstrated for me how to show that a character was in love or sad. I tried to hold a pose and Michiko burst out laughing. The three of us were having a great time until the auditorium door slammed loudly.

"What's going on here? Michiko, what are you doing?" a shrill voice asked.

I couldn't see who it was at first because of the bright stage light but looking at Michiko I could tell she knew the voice right away. Mrs. Tannabe stamped across the stage and swiftly grabbed Michiko's arm and muttered something under her breath in Japanese.

"That's enough. You need to come home now, Michiko." She turned to Michiko's uncle and spoke only Japanese to him. I could tell by their expressions that whatever it was, neither one of them was happy.

Michiko shouted, "Kudasai Mother!" (That means 'please'—I researched it.) I'm old enough to make my own decisions. I'm going to be a Kabuki actor whether you like it or not. You think you can boss me around, but I don't have to listen to you."

Mrs. Tannabe firmly crossed her arms, "We will settle this at home." She pushed Michiko ahead of her and tromped out of the auditorium, leaving Michiko's uncle with me.

I didn't know what to do. I turned off the light, "Sir, would you like a brownie? My mom made some of them for the cast party. They may have weird seeds or something in them 'cuz my mom is a pseudo Vegan, but..."

Michiko's uncle gave me a knowing look and smiled. "Oh? I am a vegan, too. I would love one. Would they happen to have tofu in them?"

Chapter Eighteen

Our friendship with Michiko changed on an unusually warm day in December. In celebration of it, Peter, Jerri and I rode our bikes home instead of begging a parent to pick us up. Michiko joined us, along with Bronson. Michiko borrowed one of Bronson's family bikes since his family was huge and they had plenty of them. I noticed that we made the shape of an arrow when we rode. Peter and Bronson rode one behind the other and we girls bicycled side by side: a plus sign of BFFs.

Ms. Phillips ran out of school calling, "Michiko, here are your grades that your mother requested."

Huh? The semester wasn't over yet. We kids knew our grades were mailed to our parents and not given to us to take home. Luckily, they arrived after the holidays so at least we'd have a little fun before the parental hammer slammed down on us.

We stopped our bikes while staring at each other. Jerri spoke up. "What's she talking about, Michiko?"

"Thank you, Ms. Phillips." Michiko looked a little sheepish. (I don't know if sheep look that way, but it's a great description.) "We are moving early back to Japan. My parents aren't getting along with each other. I'm sorry. I thought I could tell you without crying, but I can't." Michiko's eyes filled with tears. Accepting a tissue from Peter (who was always prepared for anything), she continued, "My parents don't agree on anything anymore. It's my fault. I'm one of their biggest problems. If I play the violin and study science and become whatever it is that my mother wants me to be someday, my mother will stay with us. But I can't. I am my father's daughter. My father decided to leave his sabbatical at the university to show Mother how much he cares for her. That will make Mother happy. Maybe if she is around the places and people she knows best, she'll find more to think about than me." Jamming her foot on to the bike pedal, she sped ahead leaving us behind her.

Wow, what a bomb shell. Here was Michiko with her parents on the brink of divorce and I felt hopeful for my mom and Dad. Maybe their living apart was a good idea after all.

I looked at my good friends who seemed just as shocked as I. They were real friends who I understood and trusted and who understood and trusted me back. They weren't 'after show party' pseudo-popular kids.

Straddling our bikes, with our heads hung sorrowfully, we were a pitiful sight. Everything changed in one brief moment.

I was tempted to share my parents' problems too, but it didn't seem like the best time. Besides, if I didn't talk about them, they weren't real, right?

"I don't know how serious Michiko's mother is about leaving her and Mr. Tannabe, but I've got an awesome idea to cheer up our

Pocahontas. You wanna' hear?" Bronson clapped his hands huddling us into a circle.

How could we not listen to that?

Chapter Nineteen

"Let's have a party for Michiko--a going away party." Bronson suggested. "Better yet—a surprise going away party!"

I liked surprise parties almost as much as cast parties. The fun part was planning them, you know? It was fun to figure out how to surprise the person the party was for, especially when they believed nothing was planned for them.

My goofy brother begged for a surprise party each year for his birthday. He'd say, "Are you going to have a surprise party for me this year? I have a few ideas for the theme."

I always said the same thing, "Duh, no. There won't be much of a surprise if you know ahead of time." He persisted and we let him.

Michiko was clueless that we planned a party for her. Peter's job was to ask Michiko to stay after school and help him with his science project. That would keep her out of the way in case she saw us sneaking around school getting the party ready. Jerri's job was to invite the show's cast and crew of the show and swear them to secrecy. Bronson got the decorations together because he said, "My family is so big that we're always having some sort of party." He joked, "My mother buys crepe paper streamers in bulk." My mom and I were in charge of the refreshments. No weird vegan stuff—only cookies and punch.

A couple of days before the party, I ran into Ms. Phillips as she took out her recycling to the overstuffed bins. "Ms. Phillips did you like directing the play this year?"

Her answer surprised me. "No, Beatrice I didn't. It's a hackneyed representation of the story of Pocahontas and embarrassing because of it. Everything was wrong about it—from the script to the costumes. It was embarrassing and not respectful of Indigenous people, either. But I knew that the only way we'd be allowed to do a different play next year was to prove to Principal Wells that our students want to perform good plays that are authentic. Even if the play is only a requirement for going on the New York trip, it should be good theater. Right? We're an arts magnet school. There must be a few students interested in studying drama for its own sake. Like you, for instance."

"Well, yeah you're right. I mean, I know a lot about the dramatic arts."

Oh, brother. Here goes Bumbling Bea again, I thought.

I corrected myself, "Actually, I found out I don't know much about the theater at all. I guess I thought I was an expert because my dad talks about his work so much it made me think I knew things that I didn't. Michiko knows the most about theater. Plus, she's so passionate and will do anything to be a part of it," I said.

124

"Yes, she will. Sometimes during rehearsal, I thought *she* was the director and I was the actor. Her ideas were so spot on. I'm going to miss her." Stomping on the recycling, Ms. Phillips winked at me, "Hey, I have an idea..."

I didn't think I could say no to Ms. Phillips' idea since she was the adult and all. Grown-ups don't like that much. And she did have a good idea.

Chapter Twenty

The day of the party arrived and went as planned. Michiko fell for Peter's desperate plea to help him and the cast and crew arrived quietly and hid behind Ms. Phillips desks and stuff. Even the fifth graders attended which we didn't expect 'cuz they were so obnoxious, but Bronson threatened them to behave. Bronson's decorations were a little unusual—an "It's a Boy" sign was repainted to say "Bon Voyage" but you could still see a cartoon of the naked baby under the words. He decorated with streamers that were red, purple and black.

"Black?" I kidded him as he taped them around the room.

"We had my uncle's fortieth birthday party and I guess when you're forty, people celebrate by wearing black and stuff. That's all we had 'cuz my little sister used the white streamers for Halloween when she was a mummy."

Oh, that Bronson. He was my kind of guy.

Mom did us proud. She made two kinds of cookies (tofu-free) and that great punch with the orange sherbet in it. It was awesome.

"Everybody hide," Jerri whispered loudly and we did so, trying not to talk or laugh.

Peter walked in first. I think he saw us, but he didn't let on. "Oh yeah, Ms. Phillips needs my help grading her tests..."

"Surprise!" we yelled, jumping out from wherever we were hiding.

Michiko's face burst into a smile and she giggled.

"A surprise for me?" She looked at the black balloons dangling above her. "I don't know what to say..." Michiko stammered.

Someone yelled from the back of the room, "Michiko doesn't know what to say? That's a first!"

After eating all the cookies and drinking the punch in record time, it was time for Ms. Phillips' part. "I think it's only proper that we re-enact Pocahontas and John Smith for Michiko seeing as it didn't go as planned the night of the performance. So, here goes." Ms. Phillips gestured across the room.

Out stepped Principal Wells who hid in Ms. Phillips coat closet. We all cracked up laughing at him looking pretty sweaty in a bigger version of the Pocahontas costume. Principal Wells was wearing a raven colored wig which he dramatically brushed back from his face and struck a mie pose like Michiko, squealing, "But Father, I love John Smith!"

Ms. Phillips stepped through us, now dressed in a bathrobed version of Powhatan. Speaking in a low voice, she gave us a wink,

"My dear, why are your eyes so funny? Oh, never mind. Sure, marry Mr. Smith."

On cue, the fifth grade boys threw all the red kick balls at Principal Wells (they had permission to do it one time) which knocked him to the floor as planned. "Father, I didn't know John Smith worked in a gum ball factory. That changes everything!"

It was my turn. Dressed in my now famous beard and moustache once again, I stood on a chair and recited,

'Tis almost morning, I would have thee gone—

And yet no farther than a wan-ton's bird,

That lets it hop a little from his hand,

Like a poor prisoner in his twisted gives,

And with a silken thread plucks it back again,

So loving-jealous of his liberty.

I would I were thy bird.

Sweet, so would we,

At that point I changed the Shakespeare's passage a little, I admit. We turned to Michiko. As planned we knelt on one knee and said in chorus:

Good bye, good bye! Parting is such sweet sorrow,

That we shall say good bye till it be morrow"

Michiko smiled sweetly. Later I thought she cried too, because I heard a little sniffling but I wouldn't swear to it.

The room was quiet for a moment which was a miracle because we were always talking.

"Group Hug!" Michiko yelled and the cast swarmed her with the two of us in the middle. It was great.

When we settled ourselves again, we heard a voice from the back of the room. "That's from *Romeo and Juliet*, act two scene two. It's one of my favorite passages. How about you, Michie'?"

For a minute the room was silent, a nearly impossible feat for a bunch of middle school kids. We stared at Michiko's mother. Michiko stared at her mother, too. Taking one step, Michiko seemed to float back to her mother and gave her a big hug, like most middle school kids do to their parents but never want their friends to know.

Mrs. Tannabe came to the party?

"I invited her," my mom informed me. "I thought it might help them. I know I told you not to meddle in their family business but, I couldn't help it. I asked Mrs. Tannabe before I realized what I was doing..." She paused and smiled at me. "Anyway, do as I say. Not as I do,"

My mom was so cool. After she told me not to put my nose into Michiko's business, she went ahead and did it herself instead to please me. Sounded like Mom had a Bumbling Bea alter ego of her own.

Or a magnificent one.

Chapter Twenty-One

Michiko's uncle went back to Japan. Michiko never spoke about her mother's surprise visit to school or teaching me some Kabuki that day in the theater. Maybe she was embarrassed or angry at me. I guess if you don't talk about something, it's like it never happened.

I wanted to talk about our argument in the bathroom. I wanted to talk about Michiko's mother catching us all on the stage. I wanted to check on Michiko's uncle. Why did he come to the play? I wanted to talk to Michiko, but Bumbling Bea made me feel like it was a stupid idea.

Bumbling Bea whispered, *It would be tres awkward* (That's French for "very") *and "we" don't like awkward. Besides, maybe Michiko has more she wants to say about us that we don't want to hear,* I thought. So, I kept quiet and avoided Michiko as much as possible.

Nearing the end of the semester, I spent an afternoon help-ing Ms. Phillips with her classroom. She sent me to the stage to organize all the cans of paint and clean paintbrushes. That was fine with me. I loved swirling paint with a paint stick. I could see why Mom liked art so much. It was so interesting. I was playing in the paint when I felt someone standing behind me.

"How's packing going?" I fumbled for something to say keeping my back to Michiko.

"Fine, I guess. My mother has done most of it, even though my father and I try to help her. She's very inflexible. But I am stubborn, too. She wants my violin to pack, but I forgot it here after orchestra today. I didn't mean to bother you." Michiko adjusted her violin case, turning to leave.

"You didn't." I turned off the faucet in the paint sink facing her. "I mean, don't leave. I wanted to talk to you about something. Remember the party at my house?"

"Of course, it was so fun. Peter is such a good dancer." Michiko picked at the stitching on her violin case.

I clamped a lid onto a moldy paint can saying, "I thought maybe you had a crummy time after our little fight in the bathroom."

She chuckled. "Yes, the bathroom. What is it about us and a bathroom? If we ever had a heart to heart conversation anywhere else like normal teenagers, I don't think I would know what to do."

I chuckled too. Now was my big chance to make things right with Michiko. "This may be a little confusing, but I don't want you to copy me."

"I am confused. I don't copy you. I am my own person, always." Michiko picked at the threads of the violin stitching again.

132

"That's true." I agreed. "You are definitely your own person what with your cat ears and all. I mean how sometimes I speak to people. Sometimes thoughts blurt out of my brain and they keep going right on past my lips. I exaggerate or make up things to get attention. That's Bumbling Bea speaking."

Michiko looked confused. "Bumbling Bea? But that is you speaking."

"No, that's some idiot that has taken over my personality lately," I snarked and winced. Sheesh. Would Bumbling Bea ever go away?

Michiko dropped her chin, looking out over her eyebrows. She laughed. "When I first met you, I decided that you were mean and rude. I thought, Is that girl possessed? Has an alien taken over her body?'"

I sighed, "Maybe that was the case. There was a lot going on in my life that I wasn't willing to share with anyone. Anyway, be your nice self and ignore my Bumbling Bea-isms, will you? You are too good a person for weirdness."

Michiko threw her arms around me and whispered, "I was wrong about you. You are not an alien possessed girl. You are the same Beatrice that I met when I arrived here—funny, sarcastic and honest with me. I liked her then and I still like her now. So, no matter who you think you are Beatrice, I am your friend, always."

I straightened Michiko's cat ears double checking, "So, we're friends. Right?"

"Right." Michiko smiled. "And I'll write to you once a month, okay?"

Sounded good to me.

Chapter Twenty-Two

Christmas came and went. Dad wasn't with us Christmas morning which was a real big bummer, but Mom did her best to make the day fun. Grandma Percy stayed overnight, we attended an awesome movie Edmund picked out and Mom made *real* food for dinner—mashed potatoes, canned corn (which is apparently super bad for you, but sometimes you gotta be daring) and yummy beef meat loaf. Edmund and I were so psyched by the food that he didn't even create a Flag name for it.

As much fun as we had that day, we were dreading each day drawing us closer to January first—Decision Day for Mom and Dad.

On Decision Day, Dad met us at a local coffee shop. Edmund and I worried about this day for months. We tried to distract ourselves by ordering some crazy mocha, peanut butter, latte thing. It was awful tasting, but Edmund and I didn't even notice. We were nervously sipping and sipping our drinks while Dad explained to us his side of the separation.

"Mom and I married right out of college. We were quite young, full of dreams and goals. I was headed to New York to become a professional actor and director. Mom was going to pursue her art degree there. Then we became pregnant with you, Beatrice. As you know, you were born a little less than a year later." Dad smiled while pulling at his beard.

"We took one look at you and decided that although a life in the professional world of the arts would be exciting, we needed to wait and put the family first. Besides, we were beginning our professional pursuits. We had no money, no jobs and no place to live."

"Grandma and Grandpa Percy offered for us to live with them until we got our feet under us," Mom added.

"I am forty years old next year," Dad face was flush. "I have taught theater at this level for over fifteen years. I have won awards at the university level, but I need new challenges to inspire me."

"This is true," Mom explained. "Even though Dad is not living at home as we would like, he loves you and Edmund as much as the day you were born."

"More," Dad whispered, but I heard him.

Edmund leaned into Mom and took her arm, hugging it. "What about Mom?"

"I love her now more than ever. She is my best friend." Dad smiled at Mom and she smiled back.

"But at this point, we need more time apart. We aren't divorcing, but we are going to continue living apart for now. In fact, I am going back to Japan with Professor Tanabe and his family. I will serve as a visiting professor at Mr. Tanabe's theater department for next semester."

"Then you'll come home? To us. Right Dad?"

Dad played with his coffee cup, cleaning the edge where the coffee dripped. He didn't answer my question.

I think we all knew it was a question that couldn't be answered yet.

When does someone love you enough to put you before himself? Had Mom and Dad put us first? Had I done so with Michiko?

Even Bumbling Bea couldn't answer that.

Epilogue

Michiko moved back to Japan and I didn't hear from her for a long time. In fact, I thought she forgot all about me. I guess in a way I forgot about her, too. Mom told me some friendships were like that.

"People will come in and out of your life, Beatrice," Mom told me. "That doesn't mean you aren't friends anymore. They do think about you. They sort of keep you in their back pocket, like you did with Michiko's photo of her uncle. You knew it was there, but good or bad, you weren't ready to relinquish it."

My mom was so wise. Was that okay to share?

Dad spent the semester in Japan. He lived with the Tannabes. He didn't call us much, but we did get an occasional cell phone text. Personally, I don't think you can count a text as a real conversation, though. Judging from the photos he posted on line, apparently he had a great time. Lucky him.

We went on the New York trip as planned. It was even more spectacular because Bronson attended, too. We were bus seat partners which was cool. More importantly, Bronson took me to the eighth grade graduation party and guess what? Peter took Jerri! Peter had a huge crush on Jerri for a long time, but didn't know how to tell her. Well, I could have told her. I noticed he acted weird around her and he got his words all jumbled the day of the "Poison Ivy Episode" or as we lovingly called it, P.I.E.

"Let's talk about P.I.E. again, Peter."

"No, let's not, Bea. But I could go for some *real* pie. You got any at your house, Jerri?" Peter batted his eyelashes at Jerri and we'd all crack up laughing at him.

When Dad returned from Japan, he rented a small house on the block from ours and we saw him almost daily. Edmund and I were left by ourselves a lot while Mom was "having a daily chat" with Dad. When my parents spent time together at our house, they were all smiling and giggly. Whatever that means, Edmund and I don't know. At first it was weird having him so close but so far away at the same time. We adjusted.

We're still adjusting and life is okay.

I don't know if it will ever get any better.

The beginning of our first year of high school was scary. Peter, Jerri and I decided not to audition for the school play because our math homework was super hard and it took so much time to study it. I begged Peter to help me and many days after school we'd battle Geometry together. Bumbling Bea appeared several more times that fall. She ranted and raved at my family right before big tests. I noticed that my family would stay away from me on those days. My mom never scolded me for my Bumbling Bea-ness so I finally asked her about it.

"Believe it or not, I was your age once. I remember saying and doing strange things for no apparent reason. It was like frogs jumped out of my mouth over and over again. It seems to be a stage of growing up for a young person. I knew you would figure it out someday, because we all do. Your father and I thought it was better for you to embarrass yourself enough from those moments and learn from them than for us to step in and try to help. You could handle it then and you do now, too." She kissed my forehead and straightened my straggly hair. I hugged Mom back. She handed me a box and an envelope stamped with foreign postage and cool looking penmanship. I knew it was from Japan.

While pouring some milk from our refrigerator, Peter pointed at the letter, "What's that?"

"It's from Michiko. Ha! She sent me a hard copy of an email note with a photo of another Kabuki actor." I read the note aloud.

"Dear Bea,

Hi! I knew I could send this email to you through the internet, but it wouldn't be the same, right? I'm sorry I haven't written before now, but exciting things occurred when we arrived back in Japan. First, my parents never divorced of which I'm very happy. I didn't know it, but my mother was miserable living away from home. Since we moved from one university city to another, Mother never had enough time to find an artistic outlet to express herself. She says that she is fulfilled, enriched and happy now that she has joined a chamber group and teaches private violin lessons. After much negotiation between my parents, my mother has permitted me to be my uncle's apprentice. When I am not at school studying violin and science (my mother's requests), I practice with my uncle learning all the special parts of Kabuki Theater. This photo is of ME dressed as an Onegata, a female character, remember? I know I will never perform in Kabuki Theater, but at least I am sort of living my dream and following in my family's footsteps. I have learned that is what is most important."

She wrote something I didn't expect:

"I included a pair of cat ears for you. This way you'll never forget me. Thank you for being my friend even when you did not want to be. I know that I can be impossible, but you taught me a lot about what it truly meant to be a friend. I will never forget that. I am lucky. How many Japanese girls can say they have played Pocahontas and have a true friend in America? The next time you have a bad day, put on your cat ears. They'll make you happier right away. See you in the bathroom! Love, Michiko. "

I laughed as I folded Michiko's note and photo and put them in my back pocket again. They seemed most familiar to me there.

As usual, when Peter put the milk carton away he tripped over Edmund's skate board parked in front of the refrigerator. As usual, Peter spilled chocolate milk all over my new white sweater.

"Oops, sorry Beatrice," Peter said quietly.

Bumbling Bea thought it over a minute. I placed my new cat ears on my head and chuckled, "From now on Peter, I'm going to wear a rain coat when you are near milk products. At least I won't smell like a dairy."

That Michiko girl...she taught *me* how to be a friend. I'll never forget her. Neither will Bumbling Bea.

About the Author:

Deborah's grandparents were missionaries in Japan prior in the 1930's. Consequently, Deborah's mother surrounded her with people of many cultures just as her mother had she grown up. When Deborah was sixteen years old, she visited Japan and attributes the attendance to a Kabuki theatre play as the springboard for the story of Bumbling Bea. Since then, Deborah has won awards as an author, drama teacher, and director. She has directed over 250 full length productions with children and adults alike. When Deborah isn't directing, teaching or reading, she serves as hand maiden to her beloved cats. She is mother to two grown daughters who are the best of friends and a wonderful step son. She and her husband, both newly retired, live in Kansas to be near their family and are first time grandparents.

For more information about Deborah, read her blog at Dramamommaspeaks.com or her website DeborahBaldwin.net. She can be found on several social media sites including Facebook at https://m.facebook.com/BumblingBea. Contact her at dhcbaldwin@gmail.com.

About the Illustrator:

H. Russ Brown is a theatre artist/educator from Texas who teaches and works at colleges/theatres. His areas of performance expertise include acting, musical theatre, playwriting, voice/dialects, movement and stage combat. He is a certified teacher with the Society of American Fight Directors. He is also a gifted scenic, prop and costume designer as well as a highly trained and accomplished graphic artist. He holds a MFA degree in acting from Western Illinois University.

His greatest achievement, though, is his marriage to his wife, Elizabeth, and his two amazing kids, Grant and Auben.

If you would like more information about Russ, please visit his website at hrussbrown.com

Acknowledgements

First and foremost, I would like to thank my family who have read, suggested and edited *Bumbling Bea* for as many years as I can count.

I would also like to express my appreciation to author Stacey Wallace Benefiel for her expert recommendations concerning self-publishing. You were invaluable help!

As silly as it sounds, I would also like to express my sincere thanks to *all* the people, friends, students and strangers who ever listened to me share about this story over the last thirty years. Merely by listening you helped me craft its plot. I am thankful for you.

Can you do me one favor?

I'm an indie author. I rely on readers like you to review Bumbling Bea and share your thoughts with others. I'd really appreciate you writing a review about Bumbling Bea. Please post it on Goodreads and Amazon.com Thanks so much!

86648151R00086

Made in the USA
Middletown, DE
30 August 2018